Eleven
DAYS

Eleven
DAYS

by Michael Manuell

A Scholastic Press
book
from
Scholastic Australia

LEXILE™ 900

Scholastic Press
345 Pacific Highway
Lindfield NSW 2070
an imprint of Scholastic Australia Pty Limited (ABN 11 000 614 577)
PO Box 579
Gosford NSW 2250
www.scholastic.com.au

Part of the Scholastic Group
Sydney ● Auckland ● New York ● Toronto ● London ● Mexico City
● New Delhi ● Hong Kong ● Buenos Aires ● Puerto Rico

First published by Scholastic Press in 2005.
Text copyright © Michael Manuell, 2005.
Cover copyright © Scholastic Australia, 2005.
Cover design by Antart, Sydney.
Reprinted 2005

National Library of Australia Cataloguing-in-Publication entry:
Manuell, Michael 1951-.
    Eleven days.
    For children 11 years and older.
    ISBN 1 86504 621 3.
    1. Political refugees - Juvenile fiction.
    I. Title. (Series : Thumbprint thriller).
A823.3

Typeset in Jaeger.

Printed by McPherson's Printing Group, Victoria.

10 9 8 7 6 5 4 3 2   5 6 7 8/0

*This book is dedicated to
Geoff Richards, Margrete Lamond
and all my family.*

MM

1

Holidays

If I'd paid better attention in geography lessons, I would have known that, even after four hours of flying, we would still be above Australia. I might also have known that the endless emptiness we were flying over was called the Great Sandy Desert. Personally, I'd have called it the *Never-Ending* Great Sandy Desert.

We'd eaten lunch, we'd watched a movie, I'd talked to Dad, I'd gazed out of the window, I'd read my novel. I'd even counted the number of seconds the smartly-dressed young man in front of me had managed *not* to fidget. But we still had two more hours before we got to Bali.

As if reading my mind the fidgeting young man turned round and peered at me.

'Are you going to Bali?' he asked.

'That's where the plane's going,' I said.

'Of course.'

'How long are you staying?' I asked.

'I don't know.'

'You don't know how long you're going on holiday for?'

'We don't even know if they'll let us in.'

I gaped at him, and was about to ask why, when the woman next to him whispered in his ear. He smiled apologetically and turned away. The woman pushed the black hair off his forehead and kissed his cheek.

I settled back in my seat, puzzled. I wondered why this pale young man was so confused about his holiday arrangements. Maybe they weren't actually going on holiday?

Twenty minutes later someone said, 'We've reached the coast.' I looked out of my window, and sure enough, 12,000 metres below us the Never-Ending Sandy Desert had finally come to an end at a coastline of beaches and sea.

'That's the Indian Ocean', said Dad looking up from his book. 'We're leaving Australia, Isabella.'

Dad was taking me to England to visit a whole lot of relatives, some of whom he hadn't seen for eighteen years and most of whom I'd never met. I was going a long long way from home, my mum, and my brother Henry.

I kept watching as the coast faded away.

An hour and a half later we landed in Bali.

It was hot and humid and the queues through

Immigration and Customs were long and slow. The young man and the woman were ten metres ahead of us in the next queue. They were whispering urgently to each other, and kept looking around as if they expected someone to jump on them.

Then two men in uniform came and asked for their passports. The officials looked through the passports, looked at the young man and the woman, nodded to each other, then pulled them out of the line. The four of them walked across to a glass-fronted office on one side of the Arrivals Hall.

Our queue edged forward a metre. I craned my neck to see what was happening. Inside the office, a man in a short-sleeved white shirt was sitting at a desk, smoking a cigarette. As soon as the woman entered, she strode to the desk, slammed a hand onto it, and leaned aggressively towards him.

Our queue moved again, five metres this time, to a position directly opposite the office. The man behind the desk was puffing hard on his cigarette, talking and pointing at the woman. The woman was jabbing her finger back at him. I nudged Dad, who had his head buried in a guidebook. 'Look Dad, in the office there!' I hissed, but the second he looked up, a blind snapped down over the window.

'Something weird's going on, Dad,' I said, but he hadn't seen what I'd seen, so he just grunted, and went back to his book.

Bali was mad and amazing. Mad traffic for one thing. Cars, buses, motorbikes, motor scooters, animals and pedestrians stuffed into narrow lanes that had as much traffic on them as main roads back home. The lanes were also jammed with thousands of stalls, filled with sarongs and shirts, and hats and belts and watches and puppets, and people calling out 'Come and look please,' to everyone who walked past.

By the end of that first day I was a nervous wreck. I was intimidated by the stall-owners, drained by the heat, and my senses were battered to pieces by the noisy stinking traffic.

Not that everything was entirely terrible. For instance, our hotel had a swimming pool with an open-air restaurant beside it, and a drinks bar you could swim to. And even though our room wasn't nearly as nice as the pictures in the brochure, it did have an air-conditioner.

So sometime later that evening—after a swim, a poolside massage, a seafood dinner and a sunset—I relaxed at last. The next day the shopkeepers seemed funny and friendly, the heat didn't seem quite so hot, and I even managed to laugh at the crazy traffic in the tiny streets.

But it is hard to remember the details of those two days, considering what came after.

2

The First Day

The pale young man, in the same suit and white shirt, and the woman in her floral dress, were back at the airport on Friday night when we were leaving for England. They were escorted into the departure lounge by three uniformed officials who stayed with them until Dad and I were called for our plane two hours later.

I didn't see them get on the plane: the three officials must have saved them until last. And as it was after midnight by the time we took off, and as I went straight to sleep as soon as my head hit the headrest, I didn't give them another thought until I woke up a few hours later needing to go to the loo.

I climbed over Dad who was fast asleep in the aisle seat (we were in the middle section for this part of the journey), and went down to the back of the plane to the toilets. And there they were, sitting in the last two seats.

The woman was fast asleep. Her shoulder-length dark hair was covering half of her face, and her head was leaning back against the window, so that I could see the white skin of her throat.

But the young man was awake.

'So how were your days in Bali?' he asked when he saw me.

'Fine,' I said. 'How were yours?' Then I remembered the guards taking them out of the queue when we arrived, and waiting with them in the departure lounge before we left.

'Not too good, I am sorry to say. Aunt Helena and I have spent our time in government detention.'

'Detention?' I asked, shocked. 'Is that prison?'

'It could have been considerably worse,' he explained in his strong accent. 'We were in a pleasant house in a guarded compound for the duration of our stay.'

'Have you done something bad?' I blurted, then realised how undiplomatic that was. 'Look I've gotta go,' I muttered, and darted into the toilet.

On my way back to my seat a few minutes later, I was determined to be more diplomatic.

'So you didn't see any of the shops or the beaches then?' I said sympathetically. But that sounded just as bad as what I'd said earlier.

'I saw no shops, nor any beaches.'

There was another pause. Diplomatic or not, there really was only one thing I wanted to know.

'So . . . why did the Balinese lock you up?'

'The Balinese immigration authorities were responding to a request from the government of my country to arrest us,' he stated.

'I know this is a stupid question,' I said, covering myself before I started, 'but are you some sort of international criminal?'

'Of course not!'

'So why then?' I persisted.

But he turned his head away, as if I was too rude to deserve a reply, or maybe because his aunt was waking up.

'I cannot tell you,' he said at last, staring at the back of his hands. 'I have said enough.' He kept his head down. 'I beg your pardon, but I must take some rest now.'

I felt most curious as I returned to my seat.

'What you been doing?' Dad mumbled sleepily, as I climbed over him.

'Talking to someone,' I said.

He grunted, and pulled a blanket over his head.

It was bright daylight, and I'd been awake for a while, when someone over by the windows said, 'Yeh, Afghanistan.'

Dad sat up like a jack-in-the-box, grabbed my arm and said, 'Come and look, Isabella.'

He dragged me to the exit-door window at the back of the plane so we could get a better view. We were directly behind the young man and his aunt.

'Hullo again,' I said to the young man when he looked up. 'This is my Dad, Martin.'

'Pleased to meet you,' he said politely. 'My name is Leo and this is my aunt Helena.' Dad pointed out of Aunt Helena's window.

'Afghanistan,' he said.

'Yes,' she said. 'A deeply troubled place.'

'I travelled through there twenty-five years ago,' Dad explained. 'It was more peaceful in those days.'

Aunt Helena nodded thoughtfully. 'Yes . . . It is important to remember that there are worse troubles in the world than one's own.'

Then Leo stood up. 'Martin, if you wish to watch while we fly over Afghanistan, please have my seat.'

'You can come up to our seats, Leo,' I said.

Leo and I went along the aisle. No sooner had we sat down, than the first question blurted out.

'So why *did* the Balinese lock you up?'

Leo hesitated, as if unsure where to start.

'My father is the leader of the Domerian Democratic Party, the opposition party in the parliament of Domeria,' he said. 'Have you heard of it?'

'Heard of it?' I said blankly, thinking he meant his dad's political party. I'd never even heard of Domeria.

'Domeria is a small country set in the Lodo Mountains,' Leo explained. 'It is a close neighbour to the former Soviet Union, but never a part of it, due to accidents of history.'

I must have still looked blank, because he carried on.

'There were three occasions, including the time just prior to Hitler's invasion of Russia, when Soviet troops were massed at the foot of the Lodo Mountains. But a combination of both internal Soviet and external world events meant that those forces were sent elsewhere.'

I nodded, absorbing the information.

'Our tiny country could easily have been invaded. We possessed only a small army, and small police and border forces. But fate decided it was not to be so.'

I was fascinated. Here I was, sitting on a plane from Bali, flying over Afghanistan, heading for Europe, and listening to an educated young man from a country I'd never heard of (who had been locked up in Bali), talking about Hitler and invasion by Soviet Union troops. Travel was already broadening my mind. I hoped my mind was flexible enough to cope.

'A democratic republic was established in Domeria not long after the end of the Second World War. Despite some minor troubles, the democracy has remained in place until this present day.'

'Democracy is the one person one vote thing, isn't it?' I checked.

He nodded. 'Yes. But unfortunately, over the last ten years the political party that currently forms the government has taken more and more control away from the Domerian people.'

It was complicated, but the bottom line was obviously that things were going bad in Domeria because of the bad government there. And somehow this was relevant to why he and Helena were locked up in Bali.

'Go on,' I said.

'To answer your question as to why Helena and I were detained,' he continued. 'My father has spent many years demanding that our government sign the European Union treaty against the processing of illegal money. At the same time, our finance minister has been secretly making arrangements that will actually make it easier to launder illegal money within Domeria.'

'And?' I said.

'When my father's questions in Parliament got too close to the truth of the corrupt things the government was doing, and when my father got too close to finding out which government ministers would benefit personally from the corruption, they . . .' Leo took a deep breath. '. . . they arrested my father and my mother in the middle of the night.

They also sent police to arrest Helena and me.'

'But what were they saying you'd all done?'

'The government said that it was we who were doing the evil things that they were actually doing.'

'Your crooked government was saying that *you* were crooked?'

'Correct! They said that we were laundering money, when that is exactly what *they* were doing.'

I had a good idea what he was talking about but I wanted to be sure. 'Money laundering is how illegal money is made good, right?' I checked.

He nodded. 'If a person has made money from crime, he must hide the illegal origins of that money in order to spend it. This is done by transferring it electronically, and in secret, between countries, companies and banks across the world. It is done so secretly, and in such a labyrinthine way, that the criminal origins of the money are lost. The current government of Domeria is helping criminals to spend their ill-gotten money as though they had earned it honestly!'

Leo leant back against the headrest. The silence was filled with the drone of the plane's engines, and the chatter of the passengers around us.

'And this is the terrible thing that they accuse you all of doing,' I said.

'But they will not succeed,' he said fiercely.

The way he said it gave me goose bumps. I'd

never met anyone like Leo, and evil and corruption had only ever been something I saw on the news.

'So your mum and dad were arrested, but you and Aunt Helena got away?'

'The day before my parents were arrested, I was studying alone at our apartment in the capital. Early in the afternoon, Helena suddenly turned up and insisted that I come away with her for a couple of days to Belleau. Belleau is the town by a lake where we like to swim. It is just across the border, two hour's drive away from our capital city.'

The neighbouring country was only two hours' drive away? Dad and I had flown for longer than that just to get out of Australia.

'Domeria's a really tiny place, then.'

'Less than half the size of your Tasmania.'

'So you and your aunt were in another country when your mum and dad were arrested?'

'Helena is actually a family friend, and not a real aunt. But it was not an unusual situation. We go to Belleau quite often in her sports car. I like to leave our country sometimes because it is small, and my parents are well known, and consequently so am I. Helena helps me escape.'

'But how did you know not to go home?' I asked this semi-famous person I'd never heard of.

'My parents' arrest was reported in the media. I was eating breakfast with Helena in our hotel when

I read about it in the newspaper. Friends contacted us too, and warned us that we were also in danger. They insisted that we stay away from Domeria until the accusations against my parents were dismissed. We took our friends' advice and Helena booked us tickets for Australia. We thought we would be safe there.'

'But we didn't let you in?'

'We were naïve. We didn't even consider that our government would issue a diplomatic notice for our arrest and return. The Australian government sent us straight back out of the country on the next plane after we arrived. We have been travelling for many days now.'

I'd watched movies about people escaping from arrest, but I'd never imagined I'd be sitting next to them on a plane going to England.

'So are you under arrest now?'

'No. The Indonesian government agreed to hold us until seats were available to Europe. But we are free now, at least until we get to England. We don't know what will happen when we get there . . . But I was sorry not to see Australia.'

'Did you know we're actually one of the oldest democracies in the world?' I asked him.

'I do,' he replied. 'I studied your House of Representatives and your Senate committee system in political science at school.'

That shut me up.

I was a bit overawed by Leo. Not only was he polite, clever, serious, political and multi-lingual, he also seemed smarter than many of the adults I knew.

'How old are you?' I asked him.

'Sixteen.'

Sixteen! I swallowed hard. I was going to feel well out of my depth if all European teenagers were as sophisticated as him.

'So what are you going to do now?'

'We must continue to fight,' he said quietly.

Leo didn't look like a fighter. I knew he was clever, but he didn't look at all tough.

'It is necessary sometimes to fight, and even die for freedom.'

'A lot of freedom you'd get in a coffin!' I laughed.

But Leo didn't laugh. 'Sometimes one must sacrifice oneself so that others may be free,' he said.

'There are better ways than fighting, Leo ... It's only politics.'

'In some countries, politics can mean the difference between living and dying.'

'But what about that guy in India who got rid of the British without fighting?'

'Do you mean Ghandi?'

'Gandhi. He didn't fight, did he? And he freed the Indians.'

'He did,' Leo agreed.

'Politics is just people arguing about what they want for themselves,' I said. 'Politics is just another word for selfishness. Personally, I don't care about politics at all.'

Leo fixed his dark eyes on me. 'For good or bad, politics are the way in which we shape our world. A great English politician once said, "The only thing necessary for the triumph of evil, is for good men to do nothing". So, Isabella, one is not allowed not to care.'

3

Saturday

Aunt Helena and Leo weren't arrested at Gatwick Airport. We kept a close eye on them, but Dad and Helena had already agreed that we wouldn't appear to know each other.

'We can be of more help if we're not tangled up in the same web,' Dad said. 'I've given Helena Aunty Jane's phone number. We'll just wait to see what happens.'

We made sure they stayed ahead of us in the queues, so that Dad and I could watch every move by every Customs and Immigration officer who came anywhere near them.

Leo got through Immigration, but an officer spent a lot of time studying Helena's passport, then her face, while checking things on his computer. Dad and I held our breaths, but eventually Helena was let through the gate to join Leo, and we breathed again.

'Welcome to England, by the way, Isabella,' Dad laughed, suddenly remembering the purpose of our journey.

Dad's mum, his sister Alice, and her partner, Gary, were waiting for us outside the Arrivals gates, jammed right at the front of the crowd. I saw Nana first and nudged Dad. Nana started waving madly.

We got through the barriers, and Nana grabbed us by the arms, pulling us in, and hugging and kissing us hard. The first thing I noticed was that I was half a head taller than her now. But she still looked exactly the same—short wavy blonde hair, bright brown eyes—as when I'd seen her a couple of years ago in Australia. I still wasn't taller than Aunty Alice though. She was the same tall, slim person with her dead straight blonde hair and a fringe that brushed her eyelashes. But Uncle Gary seemed shorter, and there was more grey in his long hair.

I was so busy kissing and hugging that I didn't see what happened to Leo and Helena. As we left the terminal and dragged our cases up the ramps to the carpark, I whispered to Dad, 'Did you see where they went?'

'They got in a cab. Leave it for now.'

So we kept talking and laughing as we climbed up through the carpark, loaded our bags and ourselves into Alice and Gary's grey mini-bus, and drove off to Aunty Jane's and my cousin Samantha's house in Copthorne.

Arriving at someone's house for the first time is

always the same. There's hugging and kissing at the front door. There's showing you round the house, showing you round the garden. There's 'Isabella's sleeping here, Martin's sleeping there.' And there's 'We thought we'd just have a light lunch, and a big meal tonight,' sort of talk, so that you're totally in touch with arrangements.

After my first cup of English tea, we trooped out to the front garden and waved Alice and Gary off as they drove back to London for a meeting.

By the time we were unpacked, it was midday, which meant that it was eleven o'clock at night in Australia, and that my body clock was seriously confused after only four hours snoozing on the plane. Dad looked a bit grey. He was struggling to keep awake, too, but he'd given me a stern lecture about staying up until bedtime, so he couldn't allow himself to weaken.

To prevent me falling asleep before lunch, Samantha took me into Crawley, the big shopping centre near their place. We mooched around the shops for a bit and got home in time for Spanish omelette and green salad.

After we'd eaten, and after Dad and I had had a complete rundown on every detail of family news, and after Aunty Jane made Sam and me stand back to back to see who was the tallest (Sam won by three centimetres), Dad fell silent and started rubbing his right cheek. For those of us who know, this was a sign that he was thinking hard.

'Look everyone,' he said at last. 'I know it won't come to anything but I just have to warn you anyway.'

Nana frowned, Aunty Jane looked at Dad, and Sam gave me an enquiring look.

'When we were on the plane from Bali,' Dad continued, 'Isabella, in her usual sociable way, talked to a young man called Leo.'

Sam raised her eyebrows.

'Leo was travelling with his Aunt Helena, and Leo's mum and dad have been arrested by the government of their country. To cut a long story short, Leo and Helena are now probably being pursued themselves.'

Jane and Sam glanced at each other and back at Dad. Nana put a hand to her mouth, 'What have they done?' Nana asked.

'What they've done, I suppose, is to be members of an opposition party that is in conflict with the Domerian government.'

'Domeria?' Nana asked.

'Eastern Europe, alpine country, Lodo Mountains, fifty thousand people, democratic,' Aunty Jane said. She works as a purser on planes, and flies all over Europe and North Africa. 'Its main sources of income are tourism and banking.'

'Very impressive,' said Dad.

'We get briefing notes for all our destinations,' Jane explained. 'A short history, handy hints, what not to do in the main street, and who not to criticise out loud. Not that we've flown to Domeria in years.'

'Leo and Helena were in a neighbouring country when Leo's parents were arrested,' I said. 'A place called Belleau.'

'Otherwise they too would be in prison,' Dad said. 'The government of Domeria has issued a diplomatic request for the two of them to be detained and sent back to Domeria. Indonesia detained them, but sent them on to Britain. Australia just sent them away.'

'Why weren't they arrested when they came here?' Sam asked.

'Perhaps Britain doesn't want to get involved,' Dad suggested.

'The Domerian government is involved in laundering money,' I explained.

'So Leo and Helena are free in England now?' Sam asked.

'And I'm sure they'll be just fine,' said Dad. 'As I said, it won't come to anything. They'll have friends in England who'll help. Powerful friends, unlike us.'

It made good sense.

Then the phone rang.

Jane answered. She listened for a moment, then said, 'For you, Martin. Someone called Leo.'

4

Saturday Afternoon

Dad took the phone. 'Hello, Leo. We were just talking about you.'

Everyone's eyes were fixed on Dad. Nana was holding her right hand to her mouth again.

Then Dad said, 'Helena's been kidnapped!'

Sam looked at me, astonished.

Dad said, 'Yes .. Yes . . . Yes . . .' and then, 'Don't be silly! You would have been kidnapped too . . . No, Leo, the police. They are the people to . . . But this is England, Leo, and they didn't arrest you at the airport, did they? . . . They will look after you . . .' Dad was rubbing his cheek as he talked, trying to absorb the rush of new information. '. . . Of course I'll come with you,' he said.

There was another silence while Dad listened.

'Listen to me, Leo,' Dad said firmly. 'This is what you've got to do.' He paused while he got his thoughts in order. 'First, *don't* go back to your hotel. They'll be watching it. Second, get out of the area as quickly as possible. Keep to the busiest places you can find, and they'll have less chance of kidnapping you as well… Busy places?' Dad turned to Jane and Nana. 'What are the busy places in London?'

'The West End,' Aunty Jane said.

Nana nodded. 'Oxford Circus. Oxford Street. Regent Street. Piccadilly Circus,' Nana said.

Dad repeated the place names to Leo, then said, 'Have you got any money? … Good! Get a black cab to Piccadilly Circus, and walk around there. Down Regent Street, up Regent Street, anywhere, just keep to busy streets. Find a busy café and have something to eat … I know you don't feel hungry, but you have to eat.'

Dad looked at his watch. 'The time now is three fifteen. Phone here again in one hour. By then you'll be somewhere busy, and we'll be on our way to fetch you. Okay Leo, you're on your own now, but not for long. We'll have you somewhere safe very soon.'

Dad hung up and came back to the table.

Jane was building a pile of breadcrumbs in front of her on the tablecloth. Sam was watching her as if something about the breadcrumbs was vitally important. Nana was perfectly still. Dad sat down and held his head with his fingertips and, for the first time, I heard the sound of rain outside.

'Three men came up to them as they were leaving the hotel,' Dad said. 'Two of the men grabbed Helena and shoved her into the back of a car. The other man tried to grab Leo but he got away. And now he's beating himself up for not saving Helena.'

'Then he would have been a prisoner too,' I muttered.

'And he wouldn't have been able to phone us,' Sam said.

'We've got to work out how I'm going to get to London, find Leo, and get him out of harm's way,' said Dad. 'We also have to contact the police and tell them about Helena.'

'Oh, Martin,' Nana sighed, shaking her head. 'What have you got us into?'

'It isn't "us", Mum, it's "me". I'll keep everyone else right out of it. But Leo is young, a stranger in London, he's in danger and he needs help. God or fate or something has put him in my way.'

'What are you talking about!?' I shouted. '"Fate has put him in *your* way!?" It was me who talked to Leo on the plane. You wouldn't have noticed in a million years that something weird was going on!'

Nana raised a hand to quieten me. I shut up and folded my arms tight across my chest.

Nana spoke quietly. 'Martin, listen to me. We are your family and, as your family, what is your trouble is our trouble. Do I make myself clear?'

I looked up, thinking that Dad was going to argue with Nana, but he only said, 'Yes, Mum.'

'You'd get lost on the way *to* London,' Nana continued. 'And you're virtually a stranger yourself these days *in* London. This needs planning. We have to have something to tell Leo when he rings.'

'In fifty-five minutes,' Sam stated.

'Right!' said Dad. 'First thing, how to get to the West End.'

'I can drive you,' said Jane, 'but I'm not an expert once we get into the city.'

'Alice and Gary are experts,' said Sam.

'I'll give them a ring to see if their meeting's finished,' said Jane. 'We could meet them halfway.'

Jane went for the phone.

'I'll need a mobile,' Dad said.

'You can have mine,' said Sam. 'It's charged up, and it's got twenty pounds credit.' She ran to get it.

'You'll need a list of phone numbers,' Nana said. 'I'll organise that.'

Jane hung up. 'Alice and Gary's meeting *is* finished. They're available. They'll meet us in the East Croydon station carpark.'

'We'd better go,' Dad said. 'Mum, ring me on Sam's mobile when Leo calls.'

'I'll get my coat,' I said, standing up.

'No,' said Dad firmly.

'But you and me are the only people who know what Leo looks like,' I protested.

'You are still not coming.'

'And how exactly are you going to find Leo in a big crowd in this West place?' I asked.

'The West *End*!' Dad snapped, correcting me. He was getting cross with me for pushing him.

'Whatever!' I snapped back. 'If they're really crowded places, the people and the traffic'll be mad as anything. You'll need my eyes to find Leo.' I knew I was right, but I also knew that Dad was stubborn.

'Isabella is right,' Nana stated coolly.

'You listen to Nana,' I said, cool as well. There was no way I was being left out.

Jane was watching our battle of wills from her end of the table. Sam was supporting me silently from the doorway.

'But . . .' Dad said weakly. He was giving in.

'I would prefer that Isabella stay here, too,' said Nana. 'But you've started something, Martin, that you'll need Isabella's help to finish.'

'Oh, I don't know . . .' Dad slumped back in his chair. I knew I'd won.

'There is no alternative, Martin,' Nana said.

Dad straightened up again. 'Of course you're right. I was being stupid.' Then he looked hard at me. 'But this isn't a game, Isabella. You know that, don't you? This is serious. *Really* serious.'

'I know, Dad,' I said.

He reached across and touched me gently on the shoulder.

We hadn't noticed how heavy the rain had become until we opened the front door.

'Damn!' said Jane. Dad and I turned back to grab our coats. Sam jammed her mobile into Dad's hand and said, 'Good luck.'

Jane and I made a run for her car, while Dad ran to open the front gate.

'Bloody English weather,' said Jane, as she started the engine.

The rain clouds were making it dark. That and the pouring rain made it impossible to see more than a few metres ahead. The car windows fogged up instantly even though the demister was going full blast. The car clock showed 3.30.

The rain was teeming down, the wipers kept *swish, swish, swishing* as fast as they could go, the headlights around us sparkled in the puddles and on the streaming-wet car bodies. Everything that wasn't sparkling was dull and dark.

Stuck in the car in the dark and rain, my eyes sore and sandy from tiredness, my mind began to wander. What if the kidnappers got their hands on Leo? What if they had knives, or guns?

I felt small and young, and not nearly as smart as I usually think I am. I wished I was back safe and dry at Aunty Jane's place with Sam and Nana.

It was raining even harder when we arrived at East

Croydon station. As we pulled in, across a streaming gutter, a van flashed its lights and crawled through the rain to pull up beside us. We jumped out into the rain, and climbed into the van. With two blasts on the horn, Jane drove off.

'Where we heading?' Gary asked.

No sooner was the question out of Gary's mouth than the mobile rang. Dad started flapping and groping as he searched for the pocket where he'd put Sam's phone. He found it at last, and stared at it in the darkness, trying to see which button to press.

'Top centre button,' I said from the back seat. He finally got the phone to his ear.

'Hullo, Mum… I see… Piccadilly Circus,' he said, 'under the statue of Eros. That should be crowded enough to hide him… Good job I've got Isabella to look for him.'

Dad finished the phone call and leant forward. 'Piccadilly Circus, please, Gary!' he said.

Uncle Gary swung out of the carpark into the thick traffic.

It took ten minutes to give Alice and Gary the full background to the story.

'Domeria? Never heard of it,' Gary said.

'Nor me,' said Alice.

'Nor us,' I said.

Twenty minutes later the rain was even heavier.

27

Eleven Days

Gary was hunched over the steering wheel, the demister was going like the clappers, and Alice was wiping at the fog on the inside of the windscreen.

'Dreadful night to look for someone,' she said.

'We can't park at Piccadilly Circus,' Gary said, as we pulled up at some traffic lights. 'I'll have to drop you, drive round, and pick you up again.'

'I hadn't thought about that,' said Dad.

'I might be able to find a park by the Duke of York statue, at the bottom of Lower Regent Street.'

'That'll work,' said Alice. 'It's not far. We'll whip Leo away from under Eros, and meet you there.'

'It might be difficult to find him in a crowd,' said Dad, 'I don't know how long it'll take.'

'Are you *both* getting out, Martin?' Gary asked, doubtfully. He didn't seem to think it was a good idea.

'Yes,' said Dad. 'I didn't want Isy involved, but her eyes are better than mine, and four eyes are better than two.'

'I'll get out too,' Alice said. 'It's a bit like a thriller, isn't it?'

'Except this is real,' said Dad. 'We mustn't forget that Helena is already in serious danger. As soon as we've got Leo, we go straight to the police and let them sort it out. The sooner we find Leo, the sooner the police can find Helena.'

The rain was making the traffic crawl. If I'd

known where I was, I could have got out and walked to the statue of Eros twice as fast as the van was taking us.

At the next red light, Uncle Gary said, 'We'll be coming along Piccadilly to Piccadilly Circus. We'll swing round Eros, where I'll drop you, and then I'll head south down Haymarket. At the bottom of Haymarket I'll take a right into Pall Mall, and park somewhere near the Duke of York at the bottom of Lower Regent Street. Everyone got that?'

I nodded, even though I hadn't got it. I thought I'd just stick with Dad, who knew more about London than I did.

'I wish this traffic would give us a break,' said Gary, rubbing at the windscreen. The demisting fan was still on full, but it was almost impossible to see outside. Gary opened his side window to help clear the windows, but the rain poured in so hard, he shut it straight away.

Ten minutes later Gary said, 'We're very close.'

'What time did Nana tell Leo we'd get there?' I asked Dad.

'As soon as we could,' he said, rubbing at his window and peering out. 'Poor lad.'

The worries started again. What if Leo never made it to the Eros statue? What if the kidnappers had grabbed him as soon as he'd got off the phone to Nana? What if he'd taken a chance and gone back to his hotel to get his raincoat? What if...

'At last!' Gary shouted. 'Piccadilly Circus!'

I rubbed at my window. We were approaching a big brightly-lit intersection, where several big roads came together. Piccadilly Circus wasn't exactly as bright as daylight, but it was close. It was like a meeting place for every neon sign in the world, and there were a lot of electricity companies making a lot of money out of the light show. There were neon signs for Coke, McDonalds, Panasonic, Samsung, Sanyo, Nescafe, Carlsberg, Burger King, Kenwood, as well as the usual shop signs. And, after you added the headlights of the double-decker red buses, the trucks, the cars, the vans, and the motorbikes, it was the brightest street place I'd ever seen. But as a result, there were deep dark lanes and shadowy doorways too.

'There's Eros,' said Alice, pointing.

I wiped my window again, and saw a statue of a boy on a pedestal in the middle of a large section of footpath on the far side of the intersection,

'Bugger,' said Alice, cleaning her bit of windscreen some more.

'What?' we all said.

'Because of the rain, there's no one under Eros. Not a single soul.'

5

Saturday evening

An empty space seemed to open inside my chest, as empty as the space under Eros. 'Poor Leo,' I cried. 'They've got him after all.'

'Clever Leo,' said Alice. 'He's using his brain. We arranged to pick him up from under the statue of Eros, but he would have been stupid to stick to that plan, if he was the only one sitting there.'

My emptiness filled up a little.

'Drop us where you can, Gary,' said Dad.

'I'll stop here if you're quick,' said Gary suddenly. 'See you at the Duke of York statue. Phone me if there's a change of plan.'

Gary pulled over between a double-decker bus and a black London taxi, and Alice, Dad and I jumped out into the rain. It was like jumping into a waterfall.

We waded to the footpath as Gary turned back out into the traffic. Dad grabbed me by the hand and we ran for the shelter of a building. But we were already soaked through.

'Now, Isy,' Dad said as we shook off the rain. 'Sticking together is the number one rule. Even if you just think you *might* have seen him, tell us straightaway. It doesn't matter how many false alarms we have.'

'I think we should look for him in those doorways over there close to Eros,' I said, pointing to the lights across the road beyond the statue.

'Quick. Let's cross,' said Alice. 'The lights are with us.'

We went back out into the rain, and sloshed across the road to where the boy with the bow and wings was standing five metres in the air. Directly beyond him were the bright lights of the Criterion Theatre. People were jam-packed across the entrance, escaping from the rain.

The doorway was so jammed that there was no space for us under the awning, so we stood in the shadows to one side and carefully studied the people's faces. Leo wasn't among them. I shook my head, and moved along to the next doorway.

It was the entrance to a restaurant. People were crammed ten deep, but none of the faces were Leo's.

The doorway after that was an emergency exit from a building. It was deep and, like the other doorways, packed with people; but unlike the other doorways, it was dark except for a pale green EXIT light above the double doors at the back.

I knew straight off that Leo was there, for no better reason than that I would have hidden myself in its darkness if I'd been in trouble.

I signalled to Dad and Alice to stay back and pushed my way into the crowded doorway. I tried to act naturally, as if I was just getting out of the rain like everyone else. I knew I had to be wary, because any of the people I was squeezing past could have been a kidnapper: the fat, bearded white man in front of me; the long-haired black man at my shoulder.

I couldn't see Leo, so I wriggled deeper into the mob. I smiled, nodded, pointing towards the back of the doorway as though I had someone to meet there. A miserable man with a moustache didn't want to let me through, but when I stepped on his toe, he moved aside.

Eventually, I reached the centre of the exit doors. I took a punt, and forced my way along to the left. I reached the corner, looked down and there he was, looking like a crumpled bundle of wet rags.

Leo didn't recognise me at first: my hair was flat and wet, and the light was bad. But I said, 'It's me', and suddenly he clicked who I was, and smiled. I signalled we should stand up and get out of there.

We both surfaced. But as soon as we were standing, his pale face went even paler, and his brown eyes stared over my left shoulder. I turned my head, but my view was blocked by the wide brim of a hat.

By the time I turned back, Leo was crouched down again. 'Come on, Leo,' I said, urgently. 'We've gotta go.'

Leo shook his head.

'Let's go!' I insisted. 'The van's waiting!'

'They are there!' Leo hissed. 'In hats!'

I stood up again, and turned to where Alice and Dad stood at the front of the doorway. I couldn't fail to notice the three men in hats. Even in the dark I could tell they were looking for something.

'Those are the men who took Helena,' Leo hissed from behind me. 'They have followed me.'

My guts shrank into a knot.

'Wait here,' I croaked.

I forced myself along the exit doors to the opposite corner, and started talking about the weather to a red-haired woman with glasses and a rain-hat. While I talked, I watched the three men. They were staring hard into the crowd, probably thinking like me that of all the places in Piccadilly Circus, this was the prime place to hide.

I didn't stay with my red-haired woman friend for long. Forcing down a sickening sense of panic, with my heart thumping in my chest, I worked my way back to the front of the crowd and dragged a confused-looking Dad out of the doorway.

'What's happening?' he asked, urgently.

I had to swallow hard before any words came out. 'He's in there,' I gulped. 'Don't look now, but the three men in hats next to Alice.'

Dad glanced sideways, then nodded.

'They're the ones who kidnapped Aunt Helena.'

'Right,' said Dad.

The three men were still staring into the doorway as Dad went and surreptitiously drew Alice out into the rain.

'So what do we do now?' she asked, when we'd pointed them out.

Dad thought for a moment. 'Ring Gary,' he said. 'Keep the line open, and tell him to keep his engine running. He'll have to come fast when we need him.'

Alice started punching numbers into her mobile. Dad and I turned back to watch the kidnappers.

Two of the men were still there, but the one in a check-pattern hat was missing! I broke into an instant sweat, but I clenched my fists, forcing myself to be calm.

While Alice was giving Gary his orders, Dad and I moved back closer to the doorway. We stayed behind the remaining two men, looking for the one who'd disappeared.

Suddenly I saw the check-pattern-hat man

again. He was standing in the back left-hand corner of the doorway, exactly where I'd left Leo! He was gesticulating angrily at the other two men.

'What do we do now?' Alice asked, urgently. Dad shook his head, trying to think of something.

But I knew what we had to do. Before Dad could stop me, I pushed myself into the crowded doorway again. I had to find Leo before the man in the check-pattern hat did.

I headed for the right-hand back corner, but Check-Pattern seemed to have had the same idea. As fast as I was pushing through from the street, he was pushing across from his corner. And Check-Pattern wasn't being nearly as gentle with the crowd as I was. I had the edge on him, but it was going to be close.

Then, for a moment, Check-Pattern was blocked by two men who weren't happy about being pushed around by a man in an ugly hat, and I took the advantage.

Leo was squashed as small as possible into the right-hand corner. But as small as he was making himself, Check-Pattern wasn't going to miss him for a second. I needed a distraction right now.

I spun round to see the end of Check-Pattern's nose two centimetres away from my forehead. The light from the exit sign gave it a green glow. He was so close I could see the hairs in his nostrils bristling as he breathed. For a weird moment I even thought I recognised him.

I didn't know what to do; I was swamped with a feeling of helplessness. He was way too big for me to wrestle, and I didn't have a weapon to hit him with. But while I was cringing, trying to think of a solution, my fighting instincts suddenly took over: I raised my right knee as hard and fast as I could and slammed it into his groin.

He looked unbelievably surprised for a moment, and then agonised as he doubled over. I grabbed Leo, barged through the crowd, past the other two kidnappers who were coming to Check-Pattern's assistance, and ran out into the rain.

'I've got him, let's go!'

Alice shouted into her mobile. 'Now, Gary. As a matter of urgency!'

Leo, Alice and I ran along the footpath, past the Eros statue, to the pick-up point. Dad hung back, and as I watched, the two other kidnappers came out of the doorway. Dad blocked their way, talked to them, and pointed them in the wrong direction. Then he ran to catch up with us. Check-Pattern was just stumbling from the doorway as Gary arrived with a skid at the kerb. We piled into the van, and were away across two lines of thick Regent Street traffic in seconds.

Into a traffic jam.

'This wasn't part of the plan,' Dad growled, as we came to a stop with a bus across the intersection in front of us and cars on both sides and behind.

Leo and I were kneeling in the van, our heads down below the level of the windows. We were still no more than twenty metres from Eros.

'Try and turn out of the traffic, Gary,' Alice said, 'I don't think we should stay here.'

I sneaked a look through the window. The rain was easing, and the pavement had begun to fill with people coming out from under cover.

'We ain't going nowhere,' said Gary, tapping anxiously on the steering wheel. He looked into his rear-vision mirror, and said, 'Isn't anyone going to introduce us?'

'Leo Bruin,' said Leo, raising his head. 'I am pleased and most grateful to meet you, Gary.'

'You won't be if those men find us stuck here,' said Dad.

'There they are!' said Alice. The rain had almost stopped, and we could see the three men clearly, standing at the edge of the pavement not more than ten metres away.

'Maybe we should get out, and walk away,' said Alice.

'They won't see us in here,' said Dad.

'Get down, Leo!' I hissed. The three men were coming straight towards us. I ducked down behind the seat with Leo, while Dad, Gary, and Alice locked the van doors.

'They're walking past,' said Dad, and gave a low whistle. 'Thankyou God,' he added.

'They're coming back,' Gary groaned. I pulled my coat over my head.

'It's okay. They're going back to Eros,' I heard Alice say. Leo and I stayed where we were, on the floor of the van.

'They're looking in the doorways again,' Alice reported. 'You know, this traffic really isn't going anywhere. I think we should get out and make our escape while we can.'

'We stay where we are,' Dad said.

I lifted my head. '*You* should get out, Dad,' I said.

'What!?'

'You and Alice should get out and follow them to their car. Then we'll follow them in this car. Straight to Aunt Helena.'

'Silly idea!' said Dad.

'Bloody good idea!' said Gary.

'Helena could be rescued even tonight!' Leo said.

'You think so?' Dad said.

So while Leo and I stayed hidden, and Gary kept watch on the three men, Alice put on Dad's blue coat, Dad borrowed Gary's jacket, and they both stuck beanies on their heads. Then Alice phoned Gary's mobile, leaving the line open, and plugged in her hands-free mike and earphone. Gary's phone was in the hands-free kit in the van. With the mobile lines open, we would be in contact with Dad and Alice the whole time.

'They're having a meeting outside the Criterion Theatre,' Gary said. 'Now would be a real good time to get out.'

'We're gone,' said Alice.

Dad and Alice stepped from the far side of the van, and walked back through the jammed traffic towards Eros and the Criterion. The car behind us blasted its horn, and we saw that the traffic was moving again. We had no choice but to go with the traffic flow.

'We can see them.' Alice's voice came over the speaker in the van. 'They're having a discussion.'

'We're on the move, Alice,' Gary said. 'Keep talking. We'll drive back to you as soon as we can.'

'Okay, I heard that. We'll be fine. There are plenty of people to hide behind. It's a good thing hats aren't in fashion.'

Then there was silence from Alice. Gary signalled left, and we drove into a dark street with high walls on either side. 'If we turn left, and left again,' Gary said, 'we should get back to the bottom of Lower Regent Street. From there we can come north and pick them up.'

'Hard to see them from back here,' Alice's voice

said over the speaker. 'We're going in closer.'

There were some mumbles from Dad that we couldn't decipher.

'Yes, I see. Black coats. But there are only two of them. Where's the one in the check-pattern hat?'

More mumbles from Dad.

Gary turned left, this time into a wider street, but we were still in heavy traffic.

Alice's voice came again, more excited this time. 'You need to get back to us soon, Gary. We think two of them are leaving. The check-pattern man's disappeared, so we're watching our backs . . . Wait a minute.'

Gary turned left one more time. 'This'll work,' he said.

'Check-Pattern's returned,' said Alice's voice. 'They're looking in the doorways.'

'Bingo! Lower Regent Street,' Gary shouted. 'Hang on Alice, we're coming for you now!'

'It looks like they're going! They *are* going!' Alice's voice was urgent. 'Hurry, Gary. We're following them to their car... No, wait a minute . . . Oh no. . . They're going into the tube station. Hell! Look, we'll have to follow them. We'll phone again soon.' The phone went dead.

'Damn,' said Gary, and punched the steering wheel.

'Where will they go from here?' I asked.

'Anywhere in the whole of London,' said Gary grimly.

We'd just arrived back at Piccadilly Circus. The rain had almost stopped and the streets were full of people, but Dad, Alice and the kidnappers were nowhere to be seen.

'The Piccadilly and Bakerloo underground lines run through here,' Gary explained. 'On the Piccadilly Line they could go west to Heathrow, or north to God knows where. On the Bakerloo line they could go north through Wembley, or south across the river to Elephant and Castle. And if they connect to an overground train,' he went on, 'they could go anywhere in the whole of England, or Wales, or Scotland. Or France through the channel tunnel, or if they got off at Heathrow airport they could go anywhere in the whole world.'

Leo groaned.

I didn't like this at all. London was huge, with millions of people, millions of buildings, millions of cars. I didn't want Dad to be disappearing into so many millions of things on our first day in England. Wasn't I meant to be safe and warm at Sam and Aunty Jane's place, instead of cold and damp and scared in the back of a van?

'We'll wait for them to call us,' said Gary, glancing back at me. 'I'll find us a place to park, and a nice hot cup of tea.'

I was on our plane to England but the plane wasn't moving. I was tired, and bored, and stiff, and the plane was very crowded. People were standing in the aisles as well as sitting in all the seats. Everyone was wearing a hat except me. I knew things weren't right, but I couldn't work out what.

It took me a few seconds to realise that I was no longer on the plane, but in the van. We were still driving. The van seat had been laid back into a bed, and although I was still damp, I was comfortable. Leo was beside me.

'You awake, Isy?' Dad asked.

'Sort of. What's going on?'

'We followed them to a place called Stone Cross. Then we lost them.'

'You didn't rescue Helena, then?'

'They did not,' said Leo, from beside me.

'But we've been to the police.' Dad was trying to sound positive. 'They're on the case now.'

'It was a bit slack to lose them, Dad.' I mumbled as I slipped back to sleep.

'Yeh, it was slack,' said Dad.

6

Sunday Breakfast

A phone was ringing. Church bells were ringing in the distance, too. Someone answered the phone. The church bells kept going. Strips of daylight were slicing through the cracks in the curtains.

I wasn't in the van. I was on a mattress on a floor, in someone's pale green lounge room. There was a television in the corner, a yellow couch on one side of me, and a wooden desk with a vase on the other. Two yellow armchairs were tucked into the bay window.

I had no idea what time it was and looked around for a clock, but there wasn't one. I got up to see what was going on.

Alice, Gary and Dad were at the kitchen table drinking tea. The clock above the dresser said 8.30.

'Morning, Isy,' they said.

'Am I at your place in Gipsey Hill?' I asked Gary as Alice got up to look after some toast. He nodded. 'So what's happening? Where's Leo?'

'He's asleep in the studio downstairs,' Gary said.

Alice and Gary operated a recording studio in their basement.

I sat down, and Alice put jam, Vegemite, a knife and butter in front of me.

'Have we heard from the police yet?' I asked.

'No,' Gary answered with his mouth full.

'Toast, Isabella?' Aunty Alice asked.

'Yes, please.' I looked at Dad. 'So how come you lost the kidnappers, Dad?'

'If we knew how we lost them, we could have found them again, couldn't we?' he muttered.

'So what are we going to do?' I asked.

'We've got some ideas,' said Gary. 'But we need to check them with you and Leo first.'

Leo put his head around the kitchen door an hour later. Breakfast was over, everyone had showered, and the adults were having another cup of tea. Despite everything, Leo was smiling.

'I have slept late, unfortunately,' he said.

'Nine thirty!' I laughed. 'That's not late.'

'After what you went through yesterday, I would have slept all day,' said Gary getting up to sort out toast and coffee for Leo.

'We've had some ideas,' said Dad. 'We need to discuss them so we can put a plan of action into place. The first thing must be to get you somewhere safe. I know you want to help find Helena, but we can't risk you being kidnapped as well.'

'My first thought,' said Leo, 'is that I must return home. Domeria is the source of my problems, and if I was there I might be able to do something to have my parents released. I might even be able to find out where Helena is being held here, and effect her release too.'

Leo sounded so confident that I almost believed he could do it.

'You see,' he went on, 'I know some of the people who are behind this.'

Gary delivered breakfast things to the table. 'Brave thoughts,' he said.

'Brave thoughts, yes. But I was deluding myself. How could I hope to succeed, where my father and his colleagues have failed? I can be of no use to anyone if I am also kidnapped and imprisoned.'

He buttered a piece of toast, and stared thoughtfully at it.

'Perhaps from a hiding place, with email facilities and a phone-line, I could contact our allies in Domeria. Perhaps from such a hiding place, I might be able to elicit information from Domeria that would help us here in England.' But even as he outlined his plan, Leo was doubtful.

'That makes a lot of sense,' said Dad, trying to put a good spin on it. 'And if we know you're safe, then we'll be freer to operate, too.'

'Good,' said Alice. 'Part one of our plan is that we'll take you to Copthorne this morning, Leo. You'll be staying with our sister Jane and Isabella's cousin Samantha. That's where you phoned yesterday. Isabella's grandmother will be there too.'

Leo wiped his mouth carefully on his serviette and nodded. I could see the effort it was taking him to hold himself together.

'Part two of our plan is this,' said Gary. 'We've told the police everything we know. Which isn't much. But the advantage we have over the police is that we know what the kidnappers look like. And, because we know where we lost them, we reckon we could pick up the their trail again . . .'

'So, in short,' said Dad, 'we thought we'd organise a stakeout at Stone Cross. Do you know what I mean by a stakeout, Leo?'

'I have seen many cop shows.'

'We'll get away as soon as we're ready, then,' said Gary, getting up. 'The sooner we have you tucked away, Leo, the sooner we can get back to Stone Cross.'

'May I shower before we leave?' Leo asked.

'I'll get you a towel,' said Alice.

'And we should buy a couple more mobiles,' said Gary. 'We've got to be able to keep in touch.'

'I have my credit cards with me for the purchases,' said Leo.

Dad shook his head. 'Definitely *not*! Credit cards can be traced. You mustn't use your cards at all, Leo, until this business is sorted out . . . Hang on! Maybe that's how they traced you and Helena to your hotel.'

'I didn't use mine.' Leo frowned, thinking back. 'Perhaps Helena used hers? I didn't see it, but perhaps . . .'

Alice handed Leo a towel. 'While you're showering, I'll get you some of Gary's clothes.'

Gary's clothes on Gary look normal. Gary's clothes on Leo looked . . . unusual. Even on the plane, Leo had worn a dark business suit and open-necked white shirt. Gary, on the other hand, dressed in loose, multi-patterned cotton clothes from somewhere in Asia. The clothes fitted Leo in a baggy saggy sort of way, and turned the young businessman into a young hippie.

'Unbelievable!' said Dad.

'Unrecognisable,' laughed Alice.

The phone rang and Gary answered. 'Oh, righto. Good morning,' he said. 'It's the police,' he mouthed at us.

Gary spent the next couple of minutes nodding, and saying 'uh-huh,' and 'yes,' and 'I understand,' while we listened and tried to work out what was happening from his side of the conversation. But suddenly he said, 'I'm sorry. Look, I'll have to get back to you, there's someone banging at the front door,' and hung up.

But there wasn't anyone banging at the front door at all.

'What is it?' Alice and I asked, but Gary turned straight to Leo.

'These people who took Helena. You think they're sent by your government, don't you?'

'I know they are from the present government of Domeria,' said Leo.

Gary grabbed the van keys from the kitchen dresser. 'We've gotta go right now,' he said. 'Absolutely right now.'

We gaped at him.

'The police have given the Domerian Embassy our home telephone number,' said Gary. 'With our telephone number, the Domerian Embassy can have our address in a matter of seconds.'

We grabbed our coats and were out of the front door in a minute flat. We were in the van and out of their street in a minute and a half.

7

Sunday Lunch

Gary dropped back to the speed limit once we were out of Gipsey Hill. We were heading for the safety of Jane and Sam's place. Leo hadn't said a word since we'd leapt into the van.

'Those men could be at our house even now!' Alice hissed. 'I'm not happy about this.'

'Have you got any neighbours who can keep an eye on your place?' Dad asked.

'Good idea,' said Alice, and reached into her bag. 'I'll phone Mr Anderson.'

Alice punched a number into her phone.

'Good morning Mr Anderson, this is Alice from across the road . . . I'm well thank you. But I was wondering if you could do Gary and me a bit of a favour?'

Alice didn't give much away, just said there were some people up to no good who might come to Whiteley Road, and who might watch their house. She said she'd explain in more detail later, but she and Gary hadn't done anything illegal. It seemed that Mr Anderson was happy to help.

I watched London go by. We drove through Croydon, near where we'd done the car swap last night. We drove through heavy traffic in Purley, and past car yards in Coulsdon. After a while, the houses got fewer and larger, and the spaces between them increased. There were more trees and fields, and more leaves on the ground.

I tried to make small talk with Leo. I pointed things out that I thought were interesting. But he just stared out of the window.

We stopped at a supermarket and bought two mobile phones, and reached Copthorne at twelve thirty. Alice had called ahead, so Nana, Aunty Jane and Sam were expecting us.

Our planning meeting began at one o'clock sharp in the dining room, with drinks, cakes and sandwiches. Nana sat at one end of the table, Dad at the other, and the rest of us in between.

Alice said Dad had to be the chairperson, as he'd got us into the mess. I said that it was really my fault; Leo insisted it was his. Sam pointed out that the government of Domeria was really to blame. Alice noted the discussion in the minutes.

'Just so's our Copthorne crew know,' Dad began. 'Gary and Alice's place is out of bounds at the moment.' He went on to explain the situation.

'However,' Alice added, 'we do have a team of elderly West Indian house-watchers keeping track of the situation.'

Dad nodded. 'I assume we're all clear about what happened at Piccadilly Circus. Alice and I followed the kidnappers from there, and lost them at Stone Cross in South London. When Gary picked us up there, we drove around for another half-an-hour, but we didn't see them again. Even kidnappers have to sleep some time, I suppose.'

Leo was nodding grimly at Dad's retelling of the events.

'By then we were exhausted,' said Gary, 'and still wet from the rain. I drove home with a van of snoring carcasses.'

'Jet-lagged wet snoring carcasses,' said Sam.

'So what are you proposing to do now?' Nana asked.

'What we're proposing,' I said, 'is to go back to Stone Cross and try to pick up the trail.'

'Is that safe?' Nana asked.

'We'll do it during the day,' said Gary. 'We wouldn't want people getting lost there after dark.'

Jane agreed.

'What's wrong with Stone Cross at night?' I asked.

'It's a rough place,' Nana said, 'with a lot of run-down houses and derelict factories.'

'There's five or six big roads that feed into the centre of it,' added Gary. 'A whole lot of traffic goes through there.'

'Sounds like a lovely place to spend some of our holiday, eh, Isabella?' said Dad.

'Perfect,' I agreed.

'So who's coming to Stone Cross?' Dad asked.

'We know Leo can't go anywhere,' I said.

'I must remain out of sight for now,' added Leo.

'And you can't stay here by yourself,' said Nana. 'So I'll stay here with you. I'll wash your clothes too. You'll be less conspicuous in your own clothes.'

'I'm flying to Barcelona and back today,' said Jane. 'But after this evening, I'm rostered off for a week.'

'What about Sam?' Dad asked Aunty Jane. 'Can she come with us? We'll keep her right out of danger, but another pair of eyes would be invaluable.'

'Of course I'm coming,' Sam said.

'Of course you are, Sam,' Jane smiled.

'So we're agreed. We'll go and have a careful look for these men. If and when we find them, we'll hand the whole problem over to the police. Then Isabella and I can begin our holiday. Okay with you, Leo?' Dad asked.

'I am once again overwhelmed by your generosity.'

'So that's Alice, Gary, Isabella, Samantha and me,' said Dad.

'I always look for kidnappers on Sundays,' said Sam as we got up. "Five in search of kidnappers." Sounds like a kid's adventure story to me.'

'I wish it was just a story,' I said. I'd kneed that kidnapper in the groin last night, and I never wanted to see him again. If a storybook gets too scary, you can close it up and shove it back on the shelf. But Aunt Helena was still lost, so we couldn't put our story away just yet.

Dad came round the table and gave me a hug. 'We'll be right, Isy,' he said. 'We'll keep completely out of sight. We're just five pairs of eyes watching from afar. As soon as we sight them, we're straight to the police. No danger.'

8

Sunday Afternoon

On the road again. It was a two-hour drive from Copthorne to Stone Cross, so Sam and I pushed the backs of our seats down, and lazed back, gazing up through the sunroof.

Bare tree branches and an occasional bird flashed by.

My mind drifted. I wondered what Mum and Henry were up to. Eating dinner? Watching television? Then realised they would be in bed, fast asleep. Some of my friends would still be awake though: hanging out, talking, watching videos. Watching a video would be a nice thing to do. *Life is a House* maybe, or *Centre-Stage*, or . . .

Then an idea dropped into my mind.

'Dad!'

He was slumped in the front between Gary and Alice. 'Yep?'

I sat up.

'There's a film about two people in New York that we saw.'

'We've seen a lot of films set in New York, my love. You'll have to be more specific.'

'You know the one we acted out afterwards, and Mum thought there was a Frenchman in the next room . . . A Frenchman who wants to live there, but he hasn't got a visa. So he pretends to be in a relationship with an American woman.'

'*Green Card*,' said Dad.

'That's it. What's the French actor's name?'

'Gerard Depardieu.'

My brain was speeding up. 'Dad! Dad! Do you know what I'm thinking? I'm thinking Mr Check-Pattern-Hat looked just like Gerard Depardieu.'

Dad and Alice turned to face me.

'You were close to him, Isabella,' said Alice. 'You should know.'

'I don't know why it took me so long to re-member. It seems so obvious. Big face, big nose, big man . . . except Check-Pattern-Hat had nasty eyes.'

'I wonder, Gary,' Dad said, turning back to the front. 'Is there a . . .'

'I'm reading your mind, Martin,' Gary said. 'I'll stop as soon as I see a video shop.'

We pulled up a little later in a No Parking space near a video shop on a busy road in Green Grove. Gary stayed with the van in case any traffic police came along, while we piled out.

We took an aisle each with Alice shouting out

the titles. *'Jean de Florette, Last Metro, Colonel Chabert.'*

The man at the front desk was watching us suspiciously.

'Manon des Sources,' Alice called out. *'The Machine*, look under the letter 'M' not 'T'. *My Father the Hero*'s under 'M' as well. And *Martin Guerre.'*

'What are you doing?' The man from the front desk had come to stand beside Alice as the team handed me the videos they had found.

'Looking for a video,' said Alice, smiling at him.

I looked carefully at each cover, hoping to find the picture in which Gerard Depardieu looked most like Check-Pattern-Hat.

'Are you a member?' the man asked, 'I haven't seen you in here before. In order to hire a—'

'Colonel Chabert!' I shouted. 'It's a bit old-fashioned, but it's pretty close.'

Dad took the video and showed the man.

'How much to buy this?' he asked. The man took the video, turned it over a couple of times, and said, 'Twenty quid.'

It was a battered old video, and even though twenty quid is about the same as sixty dollars in our money, Dad didn't blink, gasp, or go white. He simply handed over the money.

'Where's the nearest photocopying place?' he asked.

'Indian grocery shop, three doors down.'

Ten minutes later we were back in the van with ten enlarged photocopies of Gerard Depardieu's face from the front cover of *Colonel Chabert*. The copies weren't good, but they had to do for now.

'Has anyone got a pen or pencil?' I asked as Gary pulled into the traffic. Alice passed me a pen. I rested one of the photocopies on the London street directory, had a good long look at it, then drew a check-patterned cap on Gerard Depardieu's head.

It wasn't bad, but it wasn't right. I screwed it up and tried again. The next one was an improvement, but I screwed that up too. The third was much better: and once I'd fiddled with the pattern, and made the brim a little broader, I'd got Check-Pattern close to reality. So close, in fact, that a cold hand seemed to slide down my back.

It was another hour before we crossed the River Thames, and twenty minutes more driving to Stone Cross.

Like Piccadilly Circus, Stone Cross was a big city intersection with big roads leading onto it. Unlike Piccadilly Circus, it was dull, dirty and run-down, with decaying buildings looking down on the streams of traffic that raced round the giant roundabout at its centre. In the middle of the roundabout, in the middle of the traffic, was a dirty brown stone cross, ten metres high, surrounded by a damaged wire fence. It was not what I'd come twenty thousand kilometres from Australia to see.

We threaded ourselves into the roundabout traffic and began to circle, scrutinising the faces of the people on the pavements. The plan I had was to spot Check-Pattern straight away, follow him to where Helena was being held prisoner, release her, have Check-Pattern and his two friends arrested by the police, and then be home for dinner that night.

No such luck. After we'd been around the roundabout four times, Gary pulled into the Dover Road and parked outside some blocks of flats near a second-hand-car yard.

'Council flats,' Gary said.

We climbed out of the van, locked it, and walked back up the road. At the corner Dad pointed to an Underground sign on the far side of the roundabout.

'We came out over there.'

'The three men turned left out of the station entrance,' Alice said, 'and went across to the roundabout at the lights there.'

'Then we lost sight of them for ten seconds behind the stone cross,' Dad said. 'The lights were against us by the time we reached the crossing, but we ran across anyway.'

'We'd followed them all the way from Piccadilly Circus,' Alice grimaced. 'We weren't going to lose them the first minute we arrived.'

'They went anti-clockwise around the round-about,' Dad explained, 'and crossed again at the next lights, to The King's Arms pub over there.'

'We missed the next crossing lights too,' Alice said. 'It took us some time to get through the traffic. By the time we were across, they were gone.'

'We know they went to the left of the pub, up Dock Road,' Dad pointed. 'We ran after them, but they'd disappeared. There are a million places they could have gone.'

'Let's get away from the traffic,' Gary suggested. Four lanes of traffic were making the air pretty thick where we were standing.

'We'll get a coffee,' said Dad. 'Maybe at the shopping mall over there.' We crossed to a shabby, two-storey pink building opposite to where we'd parked the van.

The inside of the mall wasn't any smarter than the outside, but we found a teashop and ordered drinks.

'Before we go looking,' Dad said as we sat down, 'we have to set some ground rules again. Most importantly, no-one is allowed to approach Check-Pattern-Hat, or any of his associates. Not at all, for any reason. And stay in pairs. Alice and Isabella, Gary and Sam. I'll move between the pairs, but the pairs must stay together.'

'Gary and Samantha will need a copy of my drawing.' I said. 'And we'll . . .'

Alice's phone interrupted me. She answered it, listened for a moment, and said, 'Thank you Mr Anderson . . . Very helpful indeed . . . If you'd go on watching that would be a huge help . . . Don't speak to them or approach them . . . I'll call you later . . .'

Alice finished the call. 'Two men in black hats. No check-patterned hats though. They rang our doorbell at ten this morning, and have been watching from a car ever since. The resourceful Mr Anderson has also arranged for his grandson and friends to keep the surveillance going tonight.'

'As long as they're careful,' said Dad.

'They can look after themselves,' Alice said.

'They would have seen a thing or two in their time,' Gary chuckled. 'Mr Anderson senior, his grandson and their friends know how to look after themselves.'

Our drinks arrived and we gulped them down. Then we found a chemist shop and made some photocopies of my picture. I looked at it again, and wondered whether the picture really did look like Check-Pattern, or whether I was just imagining it. Nothing short of seeing Check-Pattern face-to-face again would decide how good my memory was, and that prospect didn't thrill me at all.

Armed with the photocopies, we left the mall

and headed towards The King's Arms.

'Rule number one,' Dad reminded us, 'don't approach them.'

A cold wind was blowing, it began to rain, and I wished again that I could put our story back on the bookshelf. I tried to console myself by remembering that all the thrillers I'd ever read had happy endings, and that the characters always had everything sorted out by the last page. But the problem was that our story didn't have a last page yet.

As there were only five of us to keep watch on the whole of Stone Cross, we decided to concentrate our resources on the north side, where Dad and Alice had lost track of the men the night before.

The ground we had to cover stretched from the River Thames Road in the east, to the end of Dock Road in the west, about a mile in distance, Gary informed me.

The first section, where Aunty Alice and I were watching, covered two major roads, some shops (both empty and in use), and two dark lanes that led to more public housing towers behind the shops. Sam and Gary were going to start at the far end of Dock Road, which Dad described as a combination of smashed-up houses and factory yards. Dad was going to be the link between our two teams.

We split up, and while Sam, Gary and Dad

headed east past the pub, Alice and I began patrolling our ground.

The first two shops were empty, with windows that looked like they'd been sprayed with black paint. I ran my finger down the glass and discovered the black paint was actually layers of traffic dirt.

A carpet shop was next, and because its windows were cleaner we could see the ugly carpets inside. The shop after that was called the Indian Food Café, and was sparkling clean.

A brick arch beside the Indian Food Café led into the first of the lanes that went back to the public housing towers. We peered into it, but it was so dark that we decided to wait for Dad before venturing in.

Then there was a mobile phone shop, a news-agent, and a small supermarket. The supermarket and The King's Arms were opposite each other at the start of Dock Road, the last place where the men had been seen.

Dock Road was really depressing. On the left-hand side there were terrace houses in terrible condition. The front gardens were choked with weeds and rubbish, paint was peeling from the walls, and there was either cracked or smashed glass in most of the windows. The opposite side of the street was worse. Piles of twisted metal and smashed-up wood were dumped on the dirt behind locked wire gates. The only sign of life on that side of the street was an angry dog guarding Gate 3.

We walked our route, the collars of our coats turned up against the cold wind, and peered carefully at, but steered well clear of, the few people we saw. Dad phoned us every half hour, but we didn't talk for long, in case the other team suddenly sighted Check-Pattern. The rain came and went in windy gusts, and I kept dreaming of a million places where I would rather have been.

We saw a lot of cars and a few people hurrying along. But we didn't see Check-Pattern.

It was seven thirty, and had been dark for two hours, when Dad rang.

'I've had enough,' he said. 'I'll see you at that Indian food place.'

We headed gratefully for the Indian Food Café.

Two men in turbans and brown overcoats were just leaving as Alice and I entered the fragrant warmth of the café and slumped down into chairs.

An Indian man approached our table, 'Good evening. I suspect you are hungry after all your exercise. I have watched you walking back and forth, forth and back. I am curious to know the purpose of your perambulations.'

'Don't be so nosey, Uppadhya,' the woman behind the counter said.

We ordered cups of tea, and had just finished giving Mr and Mrs Uppadhya a short version of our story as Dad entered, looking tired and depressed, followed by a grim-looking Sam and a smiling Gary.

Sam asked for the toilet, while Dad dumped himself in a chair and pushed off his shoes. Gary and Alice went to the counter to order food.

'What a complete waste of time,' Dad growled, when Gary and Alice returned.

'Bit boring if you ask me,' said Gary, stretching his arms.

'It has to be done though, Martin,' Alice said gently, reaching across to touch Dad's wrist. 'What alternative do we have? Leave Helena and Leo to the wolves and have a jolly holiday? I don't think so.'

Dad shook his head impatiently. 'Of course I don't think we should leave them to the wolves. But it really is a job for the police.' He scowled at the table.

'Listen, Dad,' I said. 'If the police come out here, they'll be looking for a man wearing an ugly hat who looks like Gerard Depardieu, except with nasty eyes. Tell me exactly what sort of chance would that give Aunt Helena?'

Dad shook his head again.

I knew that part of Dad's anger and depression was due to exhaustion. I was near dead myself. We'd flown half-way around the world, arrived yesterday, rescued Leo, lost Check-Pattern, and had just spent four hours wandering around the dirtiest, noisiest, ugliest place imaginable. And our bodies were still operating on Australian time.

Alice phoned Nana and told her our news. Nana told us that Leo was fine, that Aunty Jane would be in soon, and that she had nothing else to report.

'Let's eat and go to Mum's,' Aunty Alice said. 'We'll be able to think more clearly after a good night's sleep.'

The food came—vegetable curry, potato and pea curry, chickpea curry, naan bread and side dishes.

Mrs Uppadhya was clearing our plates away when Mr Uppadhya, who had been standing by the café window looking out into the traffic, turned and spoke to us.

'Excuse me, but what colours is the check-patterned hat for which you are searching?'

'Blue, orange, green,' I answered, 'and a bit of black.'

'A largish man with a long black coat?' Mr Uppadhya asked more urgently.

We jumped up.

'But he looks remarkably like the very famous French actor Gerard Depardieu—'

We were out of the café in a flash. Mr Uppadhya pointed along the road towards the supermarket, and Dad and I sprinted through the pedestrians, past the lane, the phone shop and the newsagent to the supermarket entrance. We looked in and couldn't see him, so we ran to the street corner opposite the pub. We still couldn't see him, and decided he must have been in the supermarket after all.

We ran back to the supermarket, and while Dad strode up and down the aisles, I stood near the checkout. But Check-Pattern wasn't in there.

We ran back onto the street.

'He's disappeared, Isy.'

'But at least someone's seen him.'

We strolled back to the Indian Café, scanning the street as we went. Gary and Sam came out from the lane to the public housing towers. They shook their heads.

Alice came up behind us. 'He didn't cross to the pub,' she said.

Mr Uppadhya beckoned to us from the café door. 'I have seen this man twice this morning,' he said, as we followed him back inside. 'He has not bought food here, but I have certainly seen him pass by my window. It did not occur to me until now that he was the same man for whom you were searching.'

We sat down at our table. Mrs Uppadhya brought over tea things, while Mr Uppadhya continued his story.

67

'But now that I have seen the hat again, I cannot believe that I did not immediately make the connection with the very same person you were seeking. I tell you, if I were this man's employer, the very first thing I would tell him, would be to get rid of that headgear. It is like a beacon in the night. It is completely recognisable and memorable.'

Mr Uppadhya threw his arms in the air, still amazed that he had failed to remember the cap.

'However, the facts of the matter show that the hat he is wearing is not such a beacon after all. Nor memorable, since I did not make any connection between it and you.' Mr Uppadhya let his arms fall to the table. 'Extraordinary,' he muttered.

'Which way does he usually come from?' I asked.

'Now there's a good question,' Mr Uppadhya said, looking back to the café window. 'Always from the right, perhaps. I did not really give him sufficient attention to be certain. But my impression would be, that he passed from the right empty-handed, and returned from the left with some purchases.'

'Mr Uppadhya, you're a dream,' said Alice, and Mr Uppadhya beamed.

'Well, it's too dark to keep looking tonight,' said Dad, looking a trillion times more cheerful. 'Let's go to Mum's place.'

Nana's flat was only twenty minutes' drive from

Stone Cross. None of us could have coped with the two-hour drive back to Copthorne, and Alice and Gary's place was still out of bounds.

We'd put our coats on, and were almost out of the door, when Dad turned back and said, 'I think one person should stay here, just in case.'

'Please,' said Mr Uppadhya, 'I am more than happy to watch the night through, if that will be of some assistance. Sleep is an inconvenience that should be avoided as much as possible.'

'I'll stay and watch with you,' Gary said. 'Two's company, and you can tell me about India to pass the time.'

It was agreed, and Alice, Dad, Sam and I walked out into the cold night, back past the lane and the shops, the bright and noisy King's Arms, and the dark car yard to the van.

I don't recall going to sleep, but I woke up in Nana's back bedroom next morning. Sam was asleep in the other bed.

9

Monday

While the rest of us slept, and while Gary and Mr Uppadhya watched at Stone Cross, Alice had spent two hours on the phone.

'I've pulled together some more family resources,' she told us next morning. 'I spoke to Aunties Joan and Doris last night, and to all the cousins I could find at short notice. I think we should be able to increase our number of watchers today by maybe six.'

The Indian Food Café was packed when we arrived. Mr and Mrs Uppadhya were flying about, delivering food and clearing crockery from the customers seated at the six tables along the left-hand wall. Two tables on the right were occupied by a group of people who I assumed were my family. Gary was serving them tea and toast, and they were all talking up a storm.

Gary said that he and Mr Uppadhya hadn't seen anything more of Check-Pattern during the night. However, they'd had an excellent all-night conversation about Mangalore, from where Mr Uppadhya had come nearly forty years ago. The two of them were looking pretty good for zero night's sleep.

Dad talked like a drain, and dragged me over to meet Aunty Joan and Aunty Doris and cousin this and cousin that, but I soon lost track of the names.

By the time I got back to Sam, who was watching by the window in case Check-Pattern came past in search of breakfast, I'd met six more rellies. And they had all come to help Leo.

Alice and Aunty Doris had put together two tables at the side of the café, and were sorting out a pile of papers, including my photocopied master-piece of Gerard Depardieu, and photocopies of the Stone Cross map from the London street directory. Dad and Mr Uppadhya were studying another map at the next table, with Mr Uppadhya pointing with a red pen, and Dad nodding and asking questions. Two of my second cousins, Susanne and Deb, were clearing cups and dishes for Mrs Uppadhya, and those who weren't talking to someone in the room, were talking on mobiles. Despite the other customers coming and going from the tables on the left-hand side of the café, we'd pretty much taken over the place.

Nana arrived fifteen minutes after us. I jumped

up and pushed through the rowdy crowd, followed by Dad and Sam. 'How's Leo?' I asked.

'Leo is still jet-lagged,' Nana said, 'and very worried about his aunt. He spent most of yesterday reading the newspapers. He's desperate for news of his parents. But there was absolutely nothing. He kept saying he should be in Domeria, and I kept saying, "under arrest?" Then he said he should be here with you looking for Helena, and I said, "getting kidnapped?" He's upset, bless him. But Jane's home today. She can take him out for a drive, to take his mind off things.'

Alice clapped her hands to get everyone's attention. 'Good morning, everyone,' she said. 'Welcome to the Indian Food Café. I'd like to introduce my brother, your nephew, your cousin, Martin, from the land down-under.'

Believe it or not, everyone applauded.

'And Isabella!' Sam shouted, and they applauded me too.

Dad raised his hands to silence them.

'As you'll appreciate,' he said, 'this was not the way I was planning to catch up with you all again after eighteen years. Not in Mr Uppadhya's café, not here at Stone Cross, not in pursuit of a kidnapper and his victim. But here we are anyway!'

Then Dad described what had been going on, starting with our plane to Bali, and ending with Mr

Uppadhya seeing Check-Pattern last night. By the time he'd finished, Aunty Doris and Alice had drawn a map of Stone Cross and stuck it on the wall. The map included a list of everybody's names, mobile numbers, and the area they were going to watch. The café was our headquarters, and Nana and Doris were in charge there. Everyone else, except for Gary, who'd fallen asleep in a chair at the back, were going to be watchers on the streets.

Copies of my picture were handed out, and we were told to phone in about anyone who might be even a slightly possible suspect. 'The point is,' Dad explained, 'Check-Pattern could have gone out yesterday and bought himself a black beanie. We cannot depend on the horrible hat alone as our means of identification.'

We were getting organised. People were checking mobiles, and sorting out hats, coats and scarves. I was ready, so I told Dad I'd wait outside. The roundabout was packed with cars, taxis and buses, and the pavement with people heading for the station.

I looked back through the window to where Dad, Alice and Doris were still showing people on their individual maps the area they had to patrol. It looked like it was going to be a while before they were ready, so I went for a walk, against the flow of the crowd, past the archway lane, past the mobile-phone shop and the newsagent, and up to the supermarket. I turned at the supermarket and flowed back with the crowd to the café again. They were still chatting inside.

I walked on, past the carpet shop, and the two empty shops. Beyond the empty shops was the entrance to the other much narrower lane, which also went back to the public housing towers.

I was just peering into it, to see where it went, when a vice-like grip clamped onto my elbow, a hand clamped over my mouth, and I was pushed inside.

Before I knew it, I was half way down the lane and through a gate in a fence. The gate slammed behind me as I was brought up face to face with a short, thin twelve-year-old boy.

'We've been watching you,' he said.

I should have been petrified, but I was so relieved not to be face-to-face with Check-Pattern that I wasn't frightened at all.

'What you up to round here?' the boy demanded.

I looked him up and down and was tempted not to answer. 'We're looking for someone,' I said anyway, yanking my elbow free.

'Who you looking for then?' the boy asked.

'We're looking for a kidnapper,' I said.

His eyes narrowed. I don't think he believed me.

'Listen!' I said. 'The aunt of a friend of ours was abducted from her hotel the day before yesterday. We followed the kidnappers to somewhere round here, but then we lost them.'

The boy scratched his nose while he considered what I'd told him. 'Why she get kidnapped?' he asked.

I gave him an outline of Domerian politics, but his only reaction was, 'You telling me the truth, girl?'

I was about to tell him I didn't have time for telling lies, or time for him, come to that, when I saw someone else out of the corner of my eye. This new someone was at least sixteen years old, very tall, and built like a stone tower.

'What's going on here, Jake my brother?' he said in lilting West Indian English.

'Hey, Rudi. She's telling me she and her people are looking for some kidnappers.'

'Kidnappers, is it?' Rudi was so cool, he sounded like he talked about kidnappers every day.

'We followed them here the night before last, and lost them,' I explained again.

'Careless girl you are, then,' he said.

'Are you also going to stand there asking questions all day long?' I demanded.

'That depends on the nature of your business, I would say. And whether or not you can keep a civil tongue in your head.'

I was thinking I would have to make a run for it, when someone called my name.

'Isabella,' said Rudi. 'That is you?'

I nodded.

Someone called again, louder and closer.

'Open the gate, Jake,' Rudi said.

Jake went and swung open the gate. Alice was standing in the opening.

'Isabella?' Alice asked, stepping back in surprise. 'Is there a problem?'

'Who are you?' asked Jake.

I could see the questions about to start all over again.

'This is my Aunty Alice,' I snapped. 'Now, are you going to back off and let us get on with our job, or are you going to waste even more of our time?' Rudi was observing me coolly. 'Or are you going to help us?' The last bit popped out of my mouth without me asking it to. Alice and the boys blinked in surprise.

'What's this accent you're speaking with?' Rudi asked. 'Sounds like *Neighbours* to me.'

'Right in one,' I said.

'So show me who you're looking for,' he said. 'Tell me how these kidnappers look now, and maybe we can spare some of our resources.'

Then Dad appeared in the gateway.

'Isabella?' he asked.

'My dad,' I said to the guys.

Everyone shook hands, and I explained that Rudi might help us. Dad immediately showed him a copy of my Gerard Depardieu picture.

'You people are trying to make a fool of me,' Rudi said. 'Why are you telling me Gerard Depardieu has been kidnapping this aunt of your friend?'

'I'm not trying to make a fool of you!' I cried. 'The main kidnapper really does look like Gerard Depardieu.'

'I seen him coming out of the shopping mall,' said Jake. 'Couldn't miss the hat.'

'A man who is wearing a hat like this needs watching,' said Rudi, tapping the picture. 'It is a danger to the eye. I'll tell you what we'll do, Aussie girl. We'll make some enquiries for you. What is the number of the mobile you're carrying?'

We gave them our mobile numbers, and told them that the Indian Food Café was our headquarters.

'I am recommending the dry potato and pea curry in that place,' Rudi nodded. 'We will be in touch if we are having some news.'

Dad's cousins Derek and Deb had the priority route from the King's Arms along Dock Road, where Check-Pattern was originally lost. Alice and Joan patrolled closer to headquarters, cruising in a circle that included the shops, River Thames Road, and the nearest public housing towers. Susanne and Dad's other cousin, Chris, had the long haul. Their territory went from the shopping mall, up the Dover Road, past the other public housing towers, past the second-hand-car yard, to Albert Road on the south side of the pub. To complete our operation, Sam, Dad and I formed the Flying Squad. We were going to respond to every sighting.

But the mobile phones didn't ring, no-one came shouting, 'We've seen him.'

I saw Rudi twice. The first time, he was patting the dog behind Gate 3 in Dock Road. The next time, he was coming out of a rusty door at the base of the stone cross. I saw Jake only once, coming out of the pink shopping mall.

Lunch was taken in shifts, with Gary and the Flying Squad filling in for those who were eating. By mid afternoon, Doris was so frustrated by our lack of success that she took to the streets too. Gary went to the underground station to watch, while Nana took care of headquarters with the Uppadhyas.

It was getting dark. Sam and I had told each other every single thing about ourselves. We'd been walking around for seven or eight hours, and still no-one had managed so much as a glimpse of

Check-Pattern. I had started to believe he was already back in Domeria with Helena.

Dad, Sam and I had stopped outside the King's Arms for the thousandth time when Dad's mobile rang. He listened for a few seconds.

'What d'you mean, Jane's here?' he spluttered. He listened some more, then started striding back to headquarters.

'Come on,' he shouted over his shoulder as he broke into a run.

Sam and I ran after him. What *was* Aunty Jane doing here, when she was supposed to be at home protecting Leo?

Back at the café, Jane looked like she was telling her story for the tenth time. Alice, Gary, Nana and Mr Uppadhya were shaking their heads in disbelief.

'I took him for a drive this morning to get him out of the house. He seemed a bit happier for it. When we got back we had lunch, and then I went into the garden to hang out some washing. When I came in again, Leo's door was shut with Sam's "Do Not Disturb" sign on it. I thought he was having a sleep. It was after lunch. People like to sleep after lunch, don't they?'

Everyone nodded as Jane went on. 'About four o'clock I thought I'd better check to see if he needed anything. He'd been asleep for three hours, and I hadn't heard a sound from him. Well, he wasn't there. The bed wasn't even creased. He must have gone while I was hanging out the washing.'

Dad grabbed his head in his hands, maybe to stop it falling apart like our plans were.

'Did he say anything this morning?' Dad asked.

'I bought him the papers again. There were pages and pages about the Middle East, but not even a line about Domeria. Leo did say at one point, "I should be there". But I just repeated that there was no point in him getting himself locked up too. I jumped in the car and drove to Three Bridges Station. I wasn't going to follow him to Domeria, but I thought maybe he might just come here.'

'You should have phoned,' Dad snapped.

'I thought I'd see if I could find him first,' Jane snapped back. 'There was no sign of him at Three Bridges, but there were any number of trains he could have caught in the previous three hours. So I drove to London Bridge Station. I wandered all over the main station and the underground platforms but there wasn't a sign of him.'

'The Northern Line would have brought him straight here from London Bridge,' Gary muttered.

'I know,' said Jane. 'But when I didn't find him I thought I'd better come here and tell you. Sorry.'

'Our family doesn't seem to be too good at tailing people,' Alice said.

'So he's gone home,' Dad said. 'There's nothing

else to think. Of course, the moment he arrives in Domeria, they'll lock him up. Silly boy.'

Everyone was silent. You could have heard a feather drop. The kidnappers and the Domerian government had won after all. It was time for my relatives to go home, and for me and Dad to start our holiday.

Then my mobile rang. The voice on the other end drove all thoughts of Leo from my mind.

'I have found the location of the man in question, Aussie girl,' said Rudi's voice. 'Meet my man Jake on the north corner of Dock Road.' And he hung up.

'Rudi's found Check-Pattern!' I shouted. 'We've got to meet Jake at Dock Road!' I ran for the door.

'Phone the others, Mum, bring them back in!' Dad shouted as we pushed out of the café.

We sprinted the hundred and fifty metres to where Jake was already waiting at the corner of Dock Road.

Jake looked at us uncertainly. 'Rudi told me to bring no more than four,' he said, and handed a piece of paper to Gary. 'You go back. Guard the door at this address. Someone might try to come out of it.'

Gary looked uncertainly at Alice.

'It's okay, Gary,' she said. 'We'll be fine.'

'Who's coming with me?' Gary asked.

'Take a young one, in case you need a runner,' said Jake.

'You go, Samantha,' Aunty Jane said. 'Isabella should go with her dad.'

Sam made a face, but nodded.

'The rest of you follow me,' said Jake.

We headed up Dock Road, and after only a couple of hundred metres, Jake turned between two of the dilapidated houses into Dock Lane. Twenty metres further on, we turned right into a smaller alley. As we left Dock Lane, a streetlight snapped on behind us, but there were no lights in the alley.

Jake led us left again, then immediately right into another alley that got darker and scungier with each step we took. The ground beneath our feet was a mixture of oily water and smashed concrete, and high brick walls loomed on either side. The alley was so narrow that I could touch the walls on both sides with my fingertips. The walls were black and slimy with trickles of water running down them.

Before long, Jake had led us around so many corners that I lost all sense of direction. Dad was looking about, trying to remember the landmarks, but he didn't have a chance.

'Where are you taking us, Jake?' Dad asked.

'To Rudi,' was all he said.

'I hope this is a good idea,' Dad muttered over his shoulder to me.

I was hoping the same thing: was it really a good idea to be following someone we didn't know, down a lot of rotting alleys in the dark?

Then the alley opened up into what looked like a half-flooded junkyard.

'Keep straight behind me,' said Jake. 'There's deep holes round here. This was a dyeing works that got bombed out in the Second World War.'

'So Rudi's got Check-Pattern?' Dad asked. I could tell he had the willies: he was scanning about him like a mad robot.

'If that's what Rudi says.'

On the far side of the dyeing works, Jake stopped.

'Wait 'ere,' he whispered, then crept away into the darkness.

We bunched around Dad. 'I don't know about this, Martin,' Jane whispered.

Dad didn't say anything. He was feeling the weight of his responsibility.

'We don't exactly know these people,' Jane added.

'And we don't exactly know where we are,' I muttered, looking around in the dark.

Rudi appeared with Jake at his heels.

'We have the location of Check-Pattern pin-pointed,' Rudi said.

'In here?' Dad hissed.

'Close by,' Rudi answered.

'Any sign of Helena?' I asked.

'No, Aussie Girl, no sign of her. But the man wouldn't be letting his prisoner be wandering about, would he now? Follow me.' Rudi turned and walked away into the blackness. Whether we could trust him or not, our fate was in his hands. We followed, and Jake followed us.

The flooded junkyard narrowed down into another alley, and then into a passage with a roof high above us. The end of the passage opened out to another dripping, flooded courtyard with no roof and gaping doorways in the walls above our heads. There would have been floors up there once upon a time, before the building was bombed out. My eyes had adjusted to the pale light that was reflecting from the clouds above us.

Rudi stopped. 'Wait here,' he ordered. 'I am going to check the situation.'

While Jane, Dad, Alice and I waited, Jake trotted back along the passage we'd just walked through. We watched Rudi pass like a shadow along the walls. At intervals, he stopped and talked to deeper shadows. After three stops, he circled back to us.

'I am told Mr Check-Pattern is still within the walls of this building. If we choose to enter there,' he pointed at an opening, 'we will have to climb four flights of stairs to bring us to him at the second floor. Now I am giving you this warning. Mr Check-Pattern comes and goes from this building with the greatest of ease. There is a fire staircase in good repair that is coming out onto the street to the north-west of us here.'

'So why didn't we go that way?' I asked.

'Mr Check-Pattern has fitted some very sophisticated security devices to those fire stairs. So what I am saying to you, the way we are coming to Mr Check-Pattern's temporary residence is by a most dangerous route. It has been left unprotected because Mr Check-Pattern assumes that not even a fool would dare to enter there.'

'We're worse than fools, then,' I said, grimly. 'Because we are definitely going in.'

'This is the way we have to go,' Rudi agreed, 'if we want to take Mr Check-Pattern by surprise.'

'All of us?' Dad asked.

'There may be some benefit accruing to us in greater numbers,' Rudi replied.

'We'd better do it then, hadn't we?' I said.

'We better had, Aussie Girl,' said Rudi, and reached down to pick up a metre-long stick from the wall beside him.

'No weapons, Rudi,' Dad said urgently.

'Listen to me, father of Isabella,' Rudi said. 'You do not have to carry anything yourself, if that is offending your principles. But me and my brother, for the safety of us all, will be carrying some lengths of wood. And please God that the Check-Pattern man will be kind and helpful to us when we surprise him. But if he is not, then let us hope that our lengths of wood will be sufficient to keep the peace with him.'

Jake reappeared behind us, carrying a stick almost as tall as he was.

'No-one following,' he reported.

We had entered the building and Rudi was whispering to us. 'Now listen to me, family of Isabella. When you are in this place, you must only be walking where I am walking. Do you understand me? If you go alone, I guarantee you will be falling a long long way, probably to your death, through jagged holes in the floors and in the stairs.'

I shivered. Jane looked down at her feet. I noticed that Dad had picked up a stick for himself.

Rudi continued his instructions. 'Now concentrate on what I am saying. Jake and I will lead. When we are giving a signal, Isabella and the woman Jane will come up to us, walking *exactly* in our footsteps. When they are standing beside us, then Jake and I will go on again. Then Aunty Alice and the father of Isabella will also follow in this way. I am clear to you?'

We nodded, and Rudi turned and crossed the flooded floor to the foot of a set of stairs at the back wall. Jake followed directly behind him. We watched Rudi prod painstakingly with his stick at each tread as he began to climb. Having reached the fifth step, he turned his head and signalled for Jake to follow. Eventually they reached the top of the first flight of stairs. Rudi signalled to Jane and me.

Despite the cold, I broke into a sweat, and I had to tell my legs to stay strong and carry me forward. Jane climbed first. She seemed to have memorised precisely the steps that Rudi had taken. I followed her exactly.

Climbing stairs had never seemed so alien. As we crept up, I was fiercely aware of how my sense of balance needed to be monitored with every single movement.

After what seemed an eternity, we were crouched next to Rudi and Jake. Rudi nodded in approval, then he and Jake went on. As they reached the next turn in the staircase, I signalled for Alice and Dad to climb up and join us.

Now Rudi, Jake, Jane and I had reached the first floor. Not that there was much floor to see. It was mostly empty gaps between the beams, with blackness below. Rudi and Jake started up the next flight, and the whole process was repeated.

After that, all we had to do was climb up along a thin ledge, clinging to window bars, skirting the mounds of rubble that had fallen from the floors above, then wriggle under a beam that had smashed onto the stairs. At last we reached the second floor.

Rudi nodded towards a corridor, indicating that that was where we would find Check-Pattern. But getting there wasn't going to be any easier than getting up the stairs. Between us and the corridor a three-metre section of floor was missing.

Once again, Rudi and Jake went ahead. Holding their sticks like tightrope walkers, they balanced along the single beam that crossed the chasm.

'One slip . . .' Jane muttered.

Dad and Alice shook their heads in disbelief.

Rudi and Jake reached the far side and turned, reaching their sticks out towards us. Jane went first. Holding one end of each stick in each hand for balance, she reached the other side and slid past Rudi and Jake to stand against the corridor wall. I crossed next; then Dad; then Alice, who said a prayer before she crossed.

Rudi put a finger to his lips to keep us silent. He pointed to a door to our right, two metres from where we were standing. Four metres beyond that was the fire escape that Check-Pattern used.

Rudi signalled Jake and Dad to position themselves on either side of the door. Then he and Jane took up positions next to Dad and Jake. Then it was Alice and my turn. Rudi pointed to the piece of broken floor that we needed to avoid.

I avoided the piece of broken floor okay. But I didn't miss the loop of lino sticking up from the edge of it. In the slow-motion that happens when you're having an accident, I felt my right foot slip under the edge of the lino, and my left foot do two little hops to compensate for my right foot not keeping up, and then watched myself fall face first, CRASH! onto the floor.

Check-Pattern was out the door in a flash.

Dad and Rudi made a grab for him, but Check-Pattern thumped through them like a bulldozer, heading for the fire stairs. Rudi was pushed onto his back as Dad tripped over me and Jane fell over Dad. Alice and Jake both lunged at Check-Pattern and missed, and he was gone down the fire stairs.

'Get after him,' Dad roared as he pushed himself free.

'Don't sweat, Man,' Rudi said. 'My colleagues have the situation under control.'

'How?' Dad demanded, looking as if he was going to make a run for the fire stairs anyway.

'Patience!' Rudi insisted.

Dad wasn't feeling like being patient, but he didn't run.

Rudi turned and slid cautiously into the room. Dad followed close behind. They came out shaking their heads.

'The lady Helena is not to be found in there,' said Rudi.

'Damn!' said Jane, pushing past Dad and Rudi to look for herself. Alice turned away, shaking her head.

'But not everything is lost,' said Rudi. 'Listen.'

We looked at him.

'Listen,' he said again, pointing to the top of the fire stairs. 'I had been expecting that Mr Check-Pattern might make a break for freedom.'

From two floors down, at the bottom of the fire escape, there was the crash of a door hitting a wall, and a babble of voices erupted up the stairs. We looked at Rudi again, but he just smiled.

The noise got louder. A mob of people seemed to be climbing up through the building. We waited and watched, wondering what exactly was going on, until Check-Pattern appeared, being marched backwards up the stairs.

Two of Rudi's 'colleagues' had Check-Pattern gripped by the arms, and though Check-Pattern was stumbling on every step, they didn't seem to notice his weight at all.

Behind Check-Pattern and his escort were Gary, Derek and Chris. Sam was following.

'Turn the man round to face his accusers now,' said Rudi, and Check-Pattern's guards flipped him round and grabbed his arms again. Not that Check-

Pattern had anywhere to run to. Ahead of him were floors and stairs filled with black holes. Behind him was a wall of Dad's cousins. Father of Isabella, ask your questions of this man.'

'Where is she?' Dad asked. He was angry, smeared with dirt and looking pretty tough.

'Who?' said Check-Pattern.

Check-Pattern had given the wrong answer, and Dad didn't say anything to help him remember. Instead, he said, 'Rudi, would you and your colleagues please bring this gentleman into the room? And Derek, Chris and Gary. Isabella, you and the others wait outside.'

Check-Pattern began to look worried.

'I am the citizen of a sovereign nation,' he said. 'I have diplomatic credentials to protect me.'

Dad went into the room. The others followed with Check-Pattern.

'Close the door,' Dad said. And the door was shut in our faces.

I don't know what went on in there. Dad must have been talking very quietly, as I didn't hear a single word from him. I only heard Check-Pattern shout once. A couple of minutes later the door opened again, and Dad came out.

'She's gone,' he said. 'They flew her to Domeria by private plane at eleven last night.'

I groaned. Even though we'd warned the police,

they'd still let Helena be smuggled out of the country.

'The police should have watched the airports,' said Jane, echoing my thoughts.

'But they could not have watched every private airstrip throughout the length and breadth of England,' Alice stated.

Dad turned to Rudi. 'We'll need to get the police.'

'That is the thing to do,' Rudi nodded. 'But I am sure you will excuse my colleagues and me. Your family forces are more than a match for this miserable man.'

Suddenly, there was the sound of boots clattering up the fire stairs.

Rudi and his friends slipped away noiselessly— back over the three-metre tightrope hole and into the darkness. I didn't even have a chance to say goodbye.

Nana and Mr Uppadhya arrived at the top of the stairs with three police officers.

'I thought I had better get the authorities, Martin,' Nana said.

We'd crowded into the room where Check-Pattern was still sitting on the floor, guarded by Gary, Derek and Chris.

'I am being held by these thugs against my will,' Check-Pattern shouted at the policewoman in charge. She glanced around at our family, checking to see if we were thugs.

'I have diplomatic immunity, you must protect me!' Check-Pattern roared.

'If I could just see your passport, then, sir,' the policewoman said.

Derek and Chris helped Check-Pattern up, and he went straight to a table against the wall. He pushed some papers aside, searched beneath some plastic bags, then started scrabbling through the paper plates, cans and bottles.

'My passport!' he shouted, turning to us. 'My diplomatic passport has been taken!'

'Are you saying one of these people stole your passport sir?' asked the policewoman.

'Yes!' snapped Check-Pattern. 'Or else those black boys! There were black boys here!'

The policewoman turned to Dad. 'Is that right?'

'Yes, they led us here.'

'And who were they, sir?'

'Local lads, I think. They were fantastically helpful.'

'Do you know their names?'

Dad shrugged, 'No we didn't catch their names. Nice lads though.'

The policewoman nodded, and turned back to Check-Pattern.

'Well, sir, I've only got your word that you have diplomatic immunity. And as you are at the scene of what may be a very serious crime, I'd like you to accompany me back to the police station, where we can sort it all out.'

'You can't arrest me!' screamed Check-Pattern.

'I'm not arresting you, sir. Just asking for your help . . . Otherwise I could leave you here, sir . . . To make your own way out, sir . . .'

She turned away, and signalled to the other police officers to leave.

It didn't take long for Check-Pattern to decide.

'I will come with you,' he said, circling away from us and making for the two policemen who were blocking the door. 'But I expect to be treated according to my position as a diplomat.'

The police officers, with Check-Pattern skulking between them, headed down the fire-escape.

'Well,' Dad said.

'We've done what we could,' said Jane.

'Shame we didn't do it yesterday evening,' I said.

'It couldn't be helped,' said Nana.

Then Derek's mobile rang.

'Yes, Mum,' he said. 'Yes, I'll tell him.'

Derek turned to Dad.

'Mum says Leo's at the café asking for you.'

10

Catching Check-Pattern, whose name turned out to be Erik Booré, was not bad going for a bunch of amateurs. I mean, we weren't exactly private eyes, or spies, or whatever.

Now that it was all over, Dad and I would have been very happy to go sightseeing at Buckingham Palace, Madame Tussauds, the Tower of London or the London Eye. But that didn't happen, did it?

After the action at the dyeing factory, Dad, Leo and I were asked to go to a police station to explain what had happened. On the way, Leo apologised for the fright he'd given us by leaving Copthorne, but explained that he couldn't stand not being part of the action.

Gary and Alice dropped us off at the front doors of the police building, and Dad told them to go home as it would probably take hours, but they insisted on waiting.

The police were very polite to Leo. They called him Mr Bruin and, in the interview room, the female sergeant we'd met at the factory offered him a chair before she left, while Dad and I had to drag our own chairs to the table. We waited half an hour before anyone came to talk to us, but finally a tall dark-haired man in a dark grey suit came in, followed by the female sergeant.

'Detective Superintendent Marlowe,' the man said, shaking Leo's hand. 'I'm sorry to have kept you waiting, Mr Bruin, but we needed instruction from our Foreign Services just to make sure we handle this matter . . . appropriately.'

'Apologies are not necessary, Superintendent,' Leo said, with a small bow.

With the tape-recorder going, we told the police everything, right from the time when Leo first spoke to me on the plane. The DS said he wanted every single detail, and asked us a lot of questions— including whether we had been followed in Bali, which hadn't even occurred to me.

That first interview took two hours, and then we were left alone with a male constable for twenty minutes, until cups of tea came. The policeman carrying the tea tray was followed by an older policeman in a uniform, and DS Marlowe and the female sergeant again. The older policeman asked us more questions about certain parts of our story, then asked us to wait some more. Leo and Dad nodded, but I wanted to say I needed my bed.

A short time after that, our sergeant brought in a tall sharp-faced man and a tall blonde woman who told us they were from the Foreign Office, and would we mind answering a few more questions. I was so pooped I didn't answer, but Dad and Leo agreed, and we went through the whole thing again.

Somewhere in the middle of the interview there were shouts in the corridor outside our room. The sergeant stopped the cassette player, excused herself, and opened the door to check what was happening.

I knew who was shouting, and Leo recognised Erik Booré's voice at the same time, and got up from the table to move out of sight of the door. The Foreign Office people turned in their chairs to listen.

Erik Booré was furious, and he had chosen our section of corridor to tell the police how he felt. I wondered if he knew that Leo was standing no more than a few metres away.

'You have insulted a member of the diplomatic corps of Domeria!' Erik bellowed. 'This matter is only concerning citizens of Domeria, not the British police! You will hear more of this! There will be repercussions!'

'As we have explained already, sir,' someone said, in a strong quiet voice, 'you were at the scene of a serious crime, and you didn't have your diplomatic identification with you.'

'My passport was stolen by the black friends of those English people! They are the criminals! They should be arrested!'

Erik's voice receded down the corridor.

The sergeant shut the door again, and she and Leo came back to the table.

I realised then that Erik Booré was even more dangerous than I had first thought. Because of his diplomatic passport, Erik Booré was free to do things that most people would be slammed in prison for. Not even the British police could touch him.

It was two thirty-five in the morning when the questions finally finished. I was completely done in. They told us that Leo would be taken to a safe house, where he'd be protected until the trouble was sorted out, and that Dad and I could go home.

'Bye, then, Leo,' I said. I knew a safe house was the best place for him, but I was thinking that I might never see him again. 'I hope it's a nice place to stay,' I finished weakly.

'I am sure it will be most comfortable, Isabella,' Leo said. 'But I—'

'They'll take the best care of you, I'm sure,' Dad interrupted, zipping up his coat. 'Let's go home, Isabella. I'm almost dead.'

As Dad turned to say goodbye to the Foreign Office people, I pulled my mobile from my jacket, and slipped it into Leo's hand.

'Just in case,' I whispered.

The sergeant saw Dad and me to the front doors.

'You'll sleep well tonight,' she said, opening the doors onto the icy night air. 'You have prevented what may have been a very serious crime.'

'We prevented half of a crime, anyway,' I said, because we hadn't prevented anything happening for poor Aunt Helena.

Alice and Gary's van was parked between two police cars, and Alice and Gary were fast asleep on the back seat. Dad tapped gently on the van window.

'Even the British government thinks this business is important,' Dad said, tapping harder. 'I can't imagine we'd have people from the Foreign Office looking after us if *we* went missing.'

Alice and Gary slept on. Dad peered in at them for a moment, then thumped on the side of the van.

Gary was awake in a second.

As for me, I was asleep as soon as my head hit the cushions of the back seat.

11

Tuesday

When I woke next morning I was in the front room of Alice and Gary's place in Gipsey Hill. Now that the authorities had interviewed Erik Booré, and Mr Anderson had reported that the two watchers had gone from Whiteley Road, we thought it was safe to return.

I stayed in bed for a while, listening to the sounds of traffic and people in the street, and trying to organise the right sort of mood for the proper start to our holiday. As I lay there I sorted through all that had happened over the last three days, putting it in order in my head, and filing it away. So far, none of it had been a holiday. We hadn't asked our travel agent to book three days of kidnapping drama as an optional extra.

It wasn't that I didn't feel glad that we had helped Leo. It was a good feeling to know that, even though the world is full of billions of people who don't know each other, there are still those who will come to your assistance if you're in trouble. People like Dad and me, our family, Rudi and his 'resources'.

I was up and dressed and heading for the kitchen when there was a quiet tapping on the front door. I didn't know whether to answer it. Could Erik Booré's team have returned to keep an eye on us?

Gary came out of the kitchen.

'Wait there,' he whispered, and edged along the hall wall to the door. As carefully as he could, keeping his shadow away from the windows, he reached out and slipped the security-chain into its latch. The quiet tapping came again. Gary looked back at me.

'Tell your Dad to come out here,' he whispered.

I turned to go, when a burst of shouting came through the front door.

'Hell's bells! Are you there, Gary man? It's me, Mr Anderson, after some green bananas.'

Gary laughed and had the chain off and the front door open in a flash. A black man with cropped grey hair was standing on the front step.

'You gave us a fright, Mr Anderson,' Gary said, letting him in. 'We didn't know who was knocking.'

'Quite right,' Mr Anderson murmured. Then in a louder voice, he said, 'Mrs Anderson was wondering whether you have any green bananas that she could borrow.'

Green bananas?

Gary closed the door.

'I thought I had better have an excuse to come visiting you, Gary,' he explained.

'Just in case someone's listening,' Gary agreed.

'Exactly! And believe me, we've been seeing plenty of watchers and listeners around your place.'

'You'd better come and give us your report then,' said Gary.

'And so is this the young lady who's stirred up so much trouble?' Mr Anderson asked as we went into the kitchen.

'Sorry about the trouble,' I said.

'Life is always trouble,' he laughed. 'Only death brings you peace.'

We sat at the table with cups of tea while Mr Anderson gave us his report.

'As I told you on the telephone,' he said. 'I am first seeing the suspicious men, two big fellows—' Mr Anderson pulled a notebook from his jacket. '—at 3.47 pm. Two men, black overcoats, black fedoras, arrive in Whiteley Road. Walk up and down street,' he read. '4.47 pm. Both men sitting in black BMW saloon.'

There was an entry for every single hour.

'I also told my grandson to make hourly entries,' he said. 'Accurate records are the basis of good detective work. The same two men are also watching your house all Monday, and into the night. Then last night at 4.15 am, my grandson is saying that two new men started watching your house, one hour and seven minutes after you were getting home.'

My stomach sank into my shoes. I had thought that the whole business was finished.

'I told my grandson and his friends they are not to come near these men,' Mr Anderson went on. 'Just to watch them watching, if you understand what I'm saying. But these new men, they are starting to try the doors. So my grandson and his friends made a lot of noise and frightened the men away.'

'I didn't hear a thing,' said Gary.

'There has been no sighting of them this morning. Mr Campbell and I have been keeping an extra careful watch. You are safe at this moment, but I am saying to you that danger will come again under the cover of the darkness.'

My holiday mood was evaporating fast.

'We have to get down to Jane and Samantha's place again, then,' Dad said.

Mr Anderson nodded. 'That is what I am advising. Don't worry your heads about this place. We will keep the watching going. We'll be making sure that there won't be no damage made, and no persons breaking in. Maybe if they are not seeing you, they will be losing their interest and taking themselves away.'

We had our stuff organised and were at the front door in nine minutes. Mr Anderson opened the door and went out to the gate carrying a plastic bag (in which Alice had put two cucumbers because she didn't have any green bananas) and looked up and down the street. The plan was that if the street was clear, he'd wave and go on his way. But if he even suspected that the watchers were back, he'd say, 'Thankyou for the bananas,' as he left.

He seemed to spend a lot of time looking down towards the park, which was the direction we had to take. I don't know how many seconds ticked away, but my heart was ticking three times as fast.

'What's happening?' Dad said, sneaking a look around the front door.

'Maybe they're back,' said Alice.

'I don't know what we do, if they are,' Gary muttered.

Just then another man came up the street and stopped beside Mr Anderson.

'Mr Campbell,' Alice whispered to me.

The two men gazed down the road.

'Come on!' I whispered. If we delayed much longer my heart was going to explode.

Mr Anderson began to raise his hand to wave, but Mr Campbell pulled it down. The watchers *were* in the street, then! Mr Anderson and Mr Campbell's heads came together, and they exchanged some hurried words. It looked like we were trapped!

But then Mr Campbell nodded, and Mr Anderson's hand shot into the air and waved.

I gasped with relief, Dad pushed me, and we were all down the garden path and into the van within a few seconds. Mr Anderson and Mr Campbell gave us a thumbs-up as we drove away.

'They may not be in the street,' Gary said, grimly, as he changed gear. 'But what's to stop them parking round the corner and following us?'

'Nothing,' I said. 'So you'll have to take a long way round to Aunty Jane's to throw them off our tail.'

'Look out the back window, Isy,' said Dad. 'We'll keep a lookout for anyone tailing us.'

All of the way to Jane and Sam's place, Dad and I took turns to watch. We were pretty sure we hadn't been followed.

Nana was still at Copthorne with Jane and Sam. They were staying together and keeping a low profile until we were certain that the men in hats no longer posed a threat.

They were full of questions, and we had to repeat every detail of what had happened since we last saw them.

For the rest of the morning, Sam and I distracted ourselves in front of the TV, apart from an hour spent discussing holiday plans with Alice, Jane and

Nana. Dad and Gary sat for a while in their coats in the front garden. Nana, Alice and Jane kept themselves busy in the kitchen, clanking saucepans and cake trays. It was a weirdly empty day.

Dinner was over, Sam and I were back in front of the TV, and the adults were in the kitchen stuffing the dishwasher, when the phone rang. I jumped in fright, which made me realise how tense I still was. Sam got up to answer it.

'Uncle Martin, it's for you,' she yelled.

Dad came in, wiping his hands on a tea towel. 'What is it now?' he said.

'It's the police,' said Sam.

Dad closed his eyes wearily as he took the phone. We turned down the TV so we could listen.

'When was that?' Dad asked, looking at his watch. 'Three hours ago.'

'What's going on?' I mouthed, but he shushed me away.

'I thought he was in a safe place!' Dad snapped. 'Being protected . . . But . . . I suppose so . . . Of course we'll keep an eye out for him . . . Of course we'll let you know if he contacts us.' Dad hung up, rubbed his eyes and muttered, 'What a bloody shambles!'

The others had already come in from the kitchen. Gary was holding a dripping sponge.

'Leo has left the safe house,' Dad said, 'and they don't know where he is.'

Nana sat down suddenly on a dining room chair. 'They were supposed to protect him!' I said.

'Safe houses are set up to keep people out, not keep people in,' Dad went on. 'They said Leo wasn't in prison.'

'But you'd think they'd keep a watchful eye on him,' said Gary.

Then the phone rang again. I glared at it. I didn't want any more bad news. Dad snatched it up. 'Leo!' he shouted after a brief pause. The way he said it meant a lot of things, like: Where the hell are you? What exactly do you think you're doing? Do you know how much you're worrying us?

'Where are you, Leo?' Dad managed to ask. 'Three Bridges Station?' He looked at Jane for help.

'It's the station nearest to us,' Jane said.

'Of course we'll pick you up. We'll be there in . . .' Dad looked at Jane again, and she held up ten fingers. 'We'll be there in ten minutes.'

Leo was waiting outside the station, looking smart, clean and calm. He had obviously got the English trains worked out. Yesterday he had found his way to Stone Cross. Today he'd found his way back from the safe house, wherever that was. But *why*?

'I have to get back to Domeria,' he said, climbing into the back seat beside me.

Jane drove off in the opposite direction to Copthorne, taking precautions against being followed.

'Not a good idea, Leo,' Dad said, crossly.

'I wish to return, nonetheless.'

'They'll arrest you the moment you fly in. What good would you be in prison?'

Dad's sharp tone showed he was pretty upset with Leo.

'I would be no good at all in a Domerian prison,' Leo admitted.

'I rest my case,' Dad said.

It was supposed to be the end of the discussion, but Leo went on. 'That is why I have come to you, Martin,' he said.

Dad looked at him. 'Meaning?' he asked.

Jane took a sharp left onto a straight and narrow country lane.

'Check behind us for anyone following,' she said, as she accelerated.

I turned and kept my eyes on the road behind while Leo explained his plan.

'Last night at the Indian Café, before we went to the police station, I spent some time talking to your cousin Derek. He drives trucks through Europe.'

'I know,' Dad said.

'He is one of the few people I have met here who knows where my country is.'

'Get to the point, Leo,' Dad growled.

'He told me that he leaves England every Tuesday night for a delivery run that takes him to within one hundred and fifty kilometres of the Domerian border.'

'One hundred and fifty kilometres is a long way,' I said.

'Derek doesn't think so,' said Leo.

'Is that someone behind us?' Jane interrupted.

High hedges blocked both sides of the lane, almost as if we were in a tunnel. Headlights had appeared behind us and were gaining. Jane accelerated some more.

'Are there exits off this road?' Dad asked.

'One. But I don't know where it goes.'

'We should take it,' I said. The headlights were getting closer.

'If they took the turn as well, we could be trapped,' Jane said. 'The turn's coming up on the right. What do I do?'

'Stay on this road,' Dad said. The inside of our car was now bright with the headlights of the following car. Leo ducked down.

'They're close!' I shouted. But as I spoke, the car dropped back and turned off to the right.

'Just someone going home,' sighed Leo.

We drove the rest of the way home in silence, but as soon as we climbed out of the car, Leo began to argue for his plan again.

'Your cousin Derek said he could drive me to the border of Domeria without any problems.'

'I see,' Dad said.

I could see it too. 'If you fly into Domeria, you'll be arrested at the airport. If you go through the road borders you'll also get locked up. But if you cross the border secretly with Derek's help . . . you maybe can contact your dad's supporters, and start sorting this whole mess out.'

'It is possible,' said Leo, turning and facing Dad.

Dad took a long look at him, then seemed to make a decision, and smiled. 'We'd better ring Cousin Derek, then,' he said.

Maybe Dad saw Leo's plan as a way of making everybody happy: Leo back in Domeria; the men in hats no longer watching us; Dad and me getting a start to our holiday at last. Perfect.

We called Derek on his mobile—he was already on the road—and it was arranged that Gary and Leo would rendezvous with him at the Clackett Lane motorway service centre on the M25, eighteen miles from Copthorne, and sixty-three miles from Dover. From Dover, the cross-channel ferry would carry them to France, from where they would drive across Europe to the Domerian border.

The Volvo's engine was running and we were crowded around the open front passenger window, puffing mist into the cold air.

'It's time to go,' Gary shouted

Leo glanced up at me. 'Isabella,' he said, 'there

are not enough words . . .' Then he ran out of words.

I couldn't manage anything myself. All the words I knew seemed to have evaporated.

'Time to go, Leo,' Gary said again. 'We don't want to miss your truck.'

'When this is over, Isabella . . .' Leo began, but suddenly he looked away.

'We're gone,' Gary shouted, and the Volvo rolled out of gate.

I was glad it was dark, so that no-one could see I was crying. I was wrung out, so I crawled into my bed in Sam's room and went straight to sleep.

I woke up when Gary came back a few hours later.

'He's on his way home,' I heard Gary say to Alice when she opened the front door. 'Just before he drove off with Derek, he said that when all the trouble is over, he will invite us to Domeria as guests of the government, and they'll give us the finest holiday we've ever had, in the most beautiful mountains in the world. Nice thought, eh?'

I slid back to sleep with a travelogue of sunlit snowy mountains playing in my head.

12

Wednesday

Dad was calling me urgently across a huge, black, broken down factory, but I couldn't see him. I was in a panic and Dad was the only person who knew the way out. I listened as hard as I could to pinpoint where his voice was coming from, but his words were echoing off the walls from every direction. Then, all of a sudden, his voice came strong and clear from just behind me. I spun around and took a step towards him. Then I was falling, and falling, and falling.

I woke and sat up straight, sweating and gasping for breath. I grabbed the doona and rubbed my face to banish the horrible images. As my breath slowed, I heard Sam snuffling in her sleep.

I knew I needed fresh air, so I slid out of bed and tried the window. It was locked, and I couldn't see how to unlock it in the dark. I crept out into the hall in search of another window. All the windows were locked, so I pulled my jacket from the coat rack, and opened the front door as quietly as I could.

The air outside was like ice. The evening mist had gone, and the moon was shining out of a clear sky, making the frosty grass sparkle.

I was wide awake because my body clock was still operating on Australian time, so I pulled on some gumboots, zipped up my jacket, and walked out onto the lawn. It was so still and quiet that all the madness of the last few days seemed to have disappeared. Standing there in the moonlight, I felt perfectly at peace.

Then a twig cracked. I jumped, then laughed quietly at myself! Silly me: the last few days had made me nervous, imagining danger under every bush. It must have been a squirrel, or a badger, or some other English animal. I listened for a few seconds, but there was nothing more. The squirrel had gone home to bed.

Within a few minutes, the fresh air and the clear night had swept the images of the nightmare factory away, and as I started to freeze I began to crave my cosy bed again.

I went back to the porch and was balancing on my left foot, tugging at the right boot, when someone grabbed my shoulder and tipped me backwards. I tried to shout, but something was clamped over my mouth and nose. I smelt something strange and lashed back with my arm. But my arm was suddenly too heavy to lift.

'Leo Bruin.'

A voice speaking in a language I didn't recognise slid into my consciousness. 'Blah Erik Booré,' it added.

'Blah blah Piccadilly Circus,' a voice replied.

Then the voices fell silent.

Was I in Gary's van? Cousin Derek's truck?

It must have been another weird dream.

The first voice woke me again, mixed up with the crackling sound of someone talking on a two-way radio. I tried to open my eyes, but my eyelids were too heavy.

One of the voices was now talking English. 'Our estimated time of arrival is in twenty minutes. Please meet us. We have a guest on board.'

Then I thought I recognised the sound of plane engines. I concentrated all my effort, and managed to open one eye a tiny crack.

I was in a small plane, lying on the floor between two pairs of seats. My feet were stuck out into the aisle. It was dark, and two men were in the pilots' seats, one row in front of me. The effort to keep my eye open became too much, so I let it close.

Then I was awake again. I opened both eyes in panic. Where was Dad? They must have put him up the back of the plane. I rolled my head sideways to look under the seats. There was no sign of him.

I knew then that I was in trouble.

'Where're we going!?' I tried to shout, but it came out as a strangled gasp.

One of the men shouted as I tried, uselessly, to get up. A face loomed down at me, and I immediately recognised him from Piccadilly Circus. His hand reached down, and the strong smell filled my nostrils again.

The next time I woke I was not on the plane anymore. I was in a blindingly bright room that reminded me of a hospital, except that there were no hospital machines or curtains around my bed.

I say I was awake, but it was sort of half-dead awake. I didn't feel scared. Although I thought I should have. It would have been the sensible thing to feel scared, but I was too tired.

I drifted in and out of sleep all through the day. At one time there was a tray of food on the table, and though I thought about eating, I couldn't be bothered to get out of bed. The next time I woke, the tray was gone.

I woke again and the room was darker, and I was unbelievably thirsty. I struggled to sit up, drank half the jug of water from the bedside table, then fell back and went to sleep again. The next time I woke I badly needed to pee.

I was as stiff as a board and my knees wouldn't

bend properly, so I rolled off the bed, and ended up sprawled on the floor.

'Come on!' I told myself fiercely.

I bent one knee, then the other, and hauled myself almost upright, but raising my head was like lifting a giant rock.

There were two doors in the room. The one opposite the window I guessed was the exit, and the other one I hoped was the bathroom. I was right.

After doing what I had to, I sat for a while, leaning my head against the white tiles, trying to feel like me again. I wasn't very successful, so I went to the sink and gave my hands and face a rough wash with icy water. That made me feel marginally more human.

I stumbled from the bathroom and shuffled to the window. I raised my eyes to look out, then stepped back in surprise. Between the metal bars, lit by a bright moon, were the best-looking mountains I had ever seen, high and sharp and covered in snow. In fact, from the pointy peaks above, right down to the road and sheds below me, everything was white. Walls of snow lined the road, and the vehicles parked beside the sheds had snow up to their windows.

Where was I? I was sure they didn't have mountains this high or snow this thick in England. And the men on the plane had mentioned Leo, Erik

Booré *and* Piccadilly Circus. I had to be in Domeria. Nothing else made sense.

My heart did a horrible leap. I had been a long way from home before, but now I was a long way from Dad as well. I took a deep breath to try to calm myself. I was close to panic, but I knew that panicking wasn't going to help me think straight.

I looked up at the moon again, remembering how Dad said that wherever you are, the same moon shines on everyone you know. So I thought of the moon shining on Dad, and shining on Mum and Henry in Sydney. I even thought of it shining on Uncle Johnny in New York. Then I smiled, remembering that it was probably also shining on Leo, right here in Domeria.

I went and sat on the bed, and pulled the covers around my shoulders for comfort. I needed to get my thoughts in order. First, I needed to know what time it was. I assumed it was still Wednesday, because I was certain I hadn't slept for more than one day since they'd kidnapped me early Wednesday morning. It was dark outside, but because it was winter, that meant it could be any time between Wednesday evening and 9.00 am on Thursday.

Then I remembered that one of the times I'd woken, there had been a tray of food on the table. It had been daylight, so the meal had probably been lunch. And because even prison guards serve meals at the proper times, it must now be before dinner-time, because there was no dinner tray sitting on the table. Unless I'd slept right through?

Then I had an unrelated idea. My room looked more like a hotel room than a prison cell, so maybe I wasn't in a prison after all. Maybe I was just in a hotel in the mountains? The important point was that in a hotel the locks are for keeping people out of your room, not for keeping you in.

I went to the door, listened for sounds, then took hold of the doorknob. As gently as I could, I tried to twist it. It turned easily. I held my breath. I kept turning until it wouldn't turn anymore. The door was definitely unlatched.

I listened again. I didn't want to open the door and find a guard standing to attention right outside. But there were no sounds. I took another breath, and gently, ever so gently, drew the door towards me. *It moved*!

I opened it until there was the smallest gap between the door and the frame. Through the gap I could see a sliver of corridor. No guards, no furniture; just some lights shining from somewhere out of sight on a polished timber floor. I pulled at the door again, but this time it jammed. I pulled harder, but it wouldn't shift. Squinting down, I could see a loop of metal on the door, with a large padlock hanging from it.

I closed the door quietly, and let the doorknob spin back slowly until it latched. So, whether or not this was a real prison, I was nevertheless still a prisoner.

I had just curled myself back into bed when I heard a noise in the corridor. There was the smallest rattle of crockery. Next, there was a rattle of keys, the sound of the padlock being removed, and then the door swung open.

I sat up.

A huge man with dark curly hair and a thick black beard filled the doorway. His broad shoulders seemed as wide as the doorframe.

'Where am I?' I asked.

He grunted and gave me a long look as if to check that I wasn't about to knock him over and make my escape while he turned to pick up the dinner tray.

'What time is it?' I asked.

He looked puzzled.

I pointed to my wrist. This obviously meant something to him. He placed the tray on the table before pulling back his shirtsleeve and thrusting a huge divers' watch at me. It said 8.45. My guess about the time had been pretty close. No wonder I was hungry.

He pointed at the tray, nodded, and left, pulling the door closed behind him. I waited until I had heard the sound of the padlock being put on again, and leapt for the table.

Food! The tray was almost overflowing. There was pumpkin soup that wasn't hot enough; dark brown bread and butter; some white cheese; and a dish of pickles. The large plate in the centre of the tray was laid out with a pile of sliced ham, a mound of cold potatoes, and a heap of sauerkraut. For dessert, they'd provided a dish of yoghurt with a swirl of honey on top. There was also a glass of white wine, which I thought was apple juice, but drank anyway. At least this wasn't one of those dry-bread-and-water sorts of prisons.

Feeling pleasantly full and surprisingly relaxed, I took a chair to the window, and sat on the back of it with my feet on the seat. The window was obviously going to be my thinking place. After my day-long sleep, I was not the least bit tired. Which was just as well, as I wanted to think things through.

The first thing I needed to know was how close to my room the guard was, and how much noise I could make before he came running. I mulled this problem over for a while.

After a lot of thought, the best idea I could come up with was for me to make a series of noises, to see at which point the guard came to investigate. I designed the test as follows:

1. Tap gently on door. Listen for someone coming. If no-one comes–
2. Tap medium hard on door. Listen, etc.
3. Bang hard on door, etc.
4. Bang very hard on door, etc.
5. Tap gently with chair on door, etc.
6. Tap medium hard with chair on door, etc.
7. Bang hard with chair, etc.

And so on until someone came, or I broke down the door and escaped anyway.

Then I realised I'd need a good excuse for making the noise. I couldn't just bang away and not have a sound reason for attracting the guard's attention. That would just make him suspicious.

I couldn't ask for soap or toilet paper because there was already plenty in the bathroom. I couldn't ask for more food, because they'd just fed me a big meal. I looked around for inspiration. The room was very bare. There were no vases of flowers, no pictures on the walls, no books or magazines. Nothing to read! I thought I could probably ask for reading material without seeming suspicious.

The secret for making the experiment a success would be to leave sufficient time between my attacks on the door. If I worked too quickly, I wouldn't know whether the guard had come because he heard the current attack on the door, or was responding to the one before.

I dragged my chair to the door and began the experiment. I was up to loudness level 6 before I got a response. When the response finally came, it came in a rush, and the padlock was undone and the door opened in a flash.

A very puzzled giant loomed in the doorway. He looked at me for a moment, then glanced down to the back of the door where I'd been bashing at it with the chair. He pointed at me to put the chair down, then bent down and rubbed his hand over the damage I'd done to the door's panelling. He raised his eyes to me again, with the same puzzled look on his face.

'How could you smash up this lovely painted door, you vandal?' his eyes asked.

I pretended not to understand, and went straight into mime mode. He glared at me while I put the palms of my hands together, and opened them like a book. Next I mimed opening a newspaper and reading it. He repeated the mimes back to me, and when I nodded and he smiled, I knew that we were communicating. He gestured to me to wait, and went out and locked the door. Ten minutes later he returned with a newspaper the size of *The Sydney Morning Herald*, and left it on the table.

I was pleased. My data proved pretty conclusively that my guard wasn't on duty nearby.

Therefore he probably wouldn't hear me if I smashed the window, squeezed through the bars, and jumped the ten metres to the ground. The only problem was, the bars were too close together, and ten metres was too far for me to jump. So there was no escape through the window, and no escape through the door.

My prison room seemed suddenly very empty.

At least I knew that Dad would be looking for me. I was certain that he'd guess I was in Domeria, and not in another slimy factory somewhere in London. My family would surely reason that Erik Booré and his mates wouldn't risk any more trouble with the English police, and so would bring me to Domeria, where I would be easier to hide.

Then I wondered where Leo was. Maybe he was still in Derek's truck zooming along the highway. Maybe he had already slipped into Domeria? I chose to think that he was somewhere safe. Simply because that made me feel less lonely.

Thinking of Leo, I settled down to distract myself through the long hours of what was going to be a sleepless night.

13

Wednesday Night

I spread the newspaper across the table. Of course it was in Domerian. Even so, I looked carefully through it from cover to cover, and I found it surprisingly interesting.

I guessed that the leading story on page one was about politics, since the main picture was of a man giving a speech to a huge crowd in a vast city square, surrounded by beautiful old buildings. People in the crowd were holding up posters and banners, and angry expressions were frozen on their faces.

The front-page story carried over to the next two pages with a column of photographs of individual people. I studied the photographs carefully, wondering whether one of them might be Leo's dad, but I couldn't find anyone who looked like Leo, or any captions with the name André Bruin. I read then re-read each of the captions, and then did the same for every other photo in the newspaper until I couldn't see straight. Then I folded the paper up, left it on the table, and went back to the window.

I still didn't know where Domeria was, although Domeria and I were both in the same place, of course. I was sure we weren't near France or Spain or Germany, because I knew where they were. We were in some mountains somewhere, probably the Lodo Mountains, which Leo had mentioned on the plane. Otherwise, I was lost.

But Dad would know where Domeria was. He absolutely, certainly, without a doubt would have got out the atlas the moment he knew I was missing, before climbing into the van, or getting onto a plane or train, to come and save me.

I wondered what Mum and Henry were doing. It was about eight or nine o'clock in the morning in Sydney, and Henry was on holidays. Maybe Mum was washing up the breakfast dishes; maybe Henry was playing with his cats, or watching television, or out on his bike. I wondered if Dad had phoned and told Mum I was missing. Or maybe he wouldn't want to worry her until he knew something definite.

Apart from the giant guard, did anyone really know where I was?

I can't have been sitting at the window for more than fifteen minutes when I heard two sets of footsteps in the corridor. I stood up, and backed myself against the wall.

There *was* someone else who knew where I was. As well as the giant, a man with close-cropped hair, in a smart suit and tie, came into the room.

'I see you are enjoying the beautiful view,' said the smart man, indicating the window as the giant closed the door. 'Peter told me he brought you today's newspaper. You have our language?'

'I looked at the pictures,' I said.

'Ah, good,' he said, watching me carefully. 'I am most sorry that you have been brought to Domeria under such difficult circumstances.'

I am definitely in Domeria then, I thought.

'But you have some information that we need before we can return you to your family.'

'Do I?' I was genuinely surprised. Did he really think I knew something so important that they would fly me all the way to Domeria? 'Things got a bit hot for you in England, did they?' I couldn't help adding.

'Perhaps,' he said. 'But it was you and your father's involvement in the domestic politics of Domeria, and your support for the Opposition party of this country, that led us to take this unusual step.'

He walked to the window and peered out into the dark, then suddenly turned and fixed his eyes on me. He was so close that I could smell his cologne.

'Once we have found out what we need to know, we will return you to your father with all speed. If we can get our answers quickly, you can be on your way immediately. Tonight.'

This was scary. It was an interrogation! I pressed

back against the wall and crossed my arms in front of my chest.

'To begin,' he said very quietly, his eyes piercing into mine. 'How long has your father been involved in the politics of Domeria?'

'He hasn't *ever* been involved in the politics of Domeria,' I said. What was this man thinking?

He laughed lightly. 'When Leo and Helena fled the country to avoid arrest for their activities, your father made contact with them in Bali.'

'I just started chatting to Leo on the plane,' I explained. 'You know how long the flight is from Australia. I didn't know him before that.'

'When Helena was brought home to Domeria for questioning, your father arranged a safe house for Leo in Britain.'

'When you kidnapped her!' I snapped. Then I wished I hadn't. I was supposed to be telling this man I wasn't involved, and here I was getting emotional.

He smiled. 'So you do admit that your organisation provided safe facilities for Leo Bruin?'

'Organisation!' I laughed. 'I've got a big family, but you wouldn't call us an organisation.'

'We know André Bruin has support from international elements. We wish to know who these people are that are trying to destabilise our country.'

'Well, don't look at me. Dad and me are supposed to be on holiday. Visiting our family.'

He shook his head and eyed me carefully. He didn't believe me. He probably thought I was a tough nut to crack. I smiled to myself, then felt stupid. How many times did I have to remind myself that this wasn't a game? This man in his smart suit was serious. My only option was to tell him the truth and make him believe it.

His next question made that option much more difficult.

'Your organisation attempted to rescue Helena. Do you deny that?'

'First, Dad and me aren't part of an organisation. We're part of a family. Second, when Leo phoned up my aunt's house to tell us that Helena had been kidnapped, we just offered to help.' His eyes narrowed. 'Third, when we picked up Leo in Piccadilly Circus—'

'How did he know how to contact you, if you had simply passed the time on a plane?'

'I gave him my aunt's phone number. You do that sometimes with people you meet.'

He lifted his chin contemptuously, and I realised immediately that he was not the sort of man who casually gave out his phone number to people he met on planes. Besides, I wasn't exactly being truthful. We gave Leo our phone number because we knew he was in trouble.

'Your organisation attempted to rescue Helena!'

he shouted, thrusting his face into mine. I jerked my head back so hard that it banged on the wall.

'There was no bloody organisation doing anything,' I shouted back at him. 'Our family helped someone who was in trouble. That's all. It is a good thing to do.'

He shook his head. Such ideas were obviously foreign to him.

'So where is Leo Bruin now?' He demanded.

'Look, mister! You've locked me up,' I said. 'How am I supposed to know anything? I don't know anything about anything, so I think you just ought to let me go home!' The last words came out as a whimper, although I was immediately ashamed of my weakness.

His eyes held me for a little while longer, then flicked away. 'We will talk again in the morning, young lady,' he said.

As he turned to leave, a question popped into my mind.

'Is Helena here?' I asked.

The man hesitated mid-stride. 'That is none of your business,' he said curtly, and left.

The funny thing was though, that as Peter the guard turned to go, he murmured 'Helena', and nodded his head.

I blinked in amazement.

14

Thursday

I had a terrible night. My body clock was so messed up it was probably on African or Antarctic time by now. I went to sleep a couple of times, but it wasn't for long because each time I woke the patch of moonlight on the floor had barely moved. And I had nasty dreams: more black factories, and shadowy gardens where I was being kidnapped.

Most of the night I just lay there, and worried and worried and worried.

Of course I was wide awake to watch the sun rising on the mountains against a mauve sky. But the beauty of it just made me sadder because my life was in such an unbeautiful mess.

I took a shower and had just got back into my pyjamas, and was wondering if breakfast was ever going to come, when keys rattled in the corridor. I hoped that it wasn't the Smart Man again, with more questions. I wasn't strong enough to face him yet. But it was Peter with breakfast. He set the tray down, looked me over carefully, then left.

At least they weren't starving me. The tray was set out beautifully. The plates and glasses and cutlery were laid on a cloth embroidered in coloured silks. There were matching fine white china bowls with lids, containing scrambled eggs and yoghurt, and plates of fruit, cheese, and bacon.

In the top right hand corner of the tray there was a cloth serviette folded into a fan shape. When I shook it out, a folded piece of paper fell from it onto the floor. I picked it up and opened it.

Handwritten in blue ink, was the following message.

> *Dear Isabella, I was extremely surprised, and somewhat dismayed, to learn yesterday that you are sharing this place of imprisonment with me. I can only surmise that Leo has involved you in some way in our troubles. This he should not have done, since the troubles of Domeria are a matter for the citizens of Domeria to solve, and should not involve external elements. I apologise for the trouble he has caused you.*
>
> *On a more practical level, the fact that you are here in the same building means that my escape plans must now include you, and will have to be reorganised*

accordingly. Rest assured this will be done
very promptly, and that you will be away
from Domeria soon.

Regards, Helena.

P.S. Please destroy this letter for the
sake of our security.

I could never have imagined how happy a folded piece of paper would make me feel. I danced around the room waving the letter in the air, and kissed it a thousand times. The window bars were no longer a barrier to me. A padlocked door was nothing! I leapt onto the bed and read the letter again to make sure I hadn't been dreaming, and the words, wonderfully, still said the same thing. I bounced on the mattress, threw the letter in the air, clapped my hands, and caught it again. But as I caught it, the impact of the last sentence suddenly hit me, and I realised the stupidity of my celebrations.

I climbed quickly from the bed, headed straight for the bathroom, shut the door and locked it. I ripped the letter into tiny pieces and flushed them down the toilet. It took two flushes to get the last six pieces to go.

Then I went back and sat on the bed and tried to remain calm.

But my excitement swelled again. Freedom!

Soon I would be free of this room! Free of Peter the Giant and the Smart Man. Soon I would be feeling snow, cold between my toes, the sharp air making my skin tingle, my breath gushing like steam.

I hesitated. Free of this room, yes. Free of my guards, yes. But out in the cold with snow between my toes? And tingling skin and steaming breath? I was still dressed in my pyjamas and zipper jacket. I needed something else to wear!

I considered the problem over breakfast. Devouring every single morsel—knowing that I had to be as strong as possible for our escape—I wondered just how that piece of paper had got into the serviette. Could Helena be spending time in prison folding laundry?

Soon after the keys rattled again. I was still so elated that I didn't even worry about whether it might be the Smart Man coming back to question me. But it was only Peter to fetch my tray.

I watched him closely. He seemed pleased that there wasn't a scrap of food left. He even checked under the dish lids and nodded at the empty bowls, as though it was important to him that I had eaten well. He lifted the serviette and gave it a shake before he laid it across the top of the crockery. Did he know about the note?

As he turned to leave, I rushed over and grabbed him by the sleeve. 'Excuse me,' I said politely, pulling at my pyjama jacket. 'I need some clothes.'

He seemed to understand straight away. He looked me up and down, as if he was working out my size, then nodded and left.

Half an hour later, he returned with a small suitcase, which he placed just inside the door. As soon as the door was locked, I sprinted for the suitcase, pulled it onto the bed and flung back the lid.

On top, folded neatly, were a woolly shirt, some thick brown woollen pants, a pair of mittens, and a pair of long red socks. The shirt was made of heavy dark brown wool, with thick yellow stitching, and woolly tassels in pale brown dangling from the tips of the shoulders. I'd never seen anything quite like it before. The pants were of a similar brown material, and tapered from a baggy top to a thin band of orange leather tight below the knee. The thick red wool socks and mittens seemed normal. There was also a pair of yellow ski boots wrapped in a padded anorak with buttons that looked like they were made out of bones. I wondered if I'd been provided with the national costume of Domeria.

The clothes were rough and scratchy but they were a good fit. I was starting to think that Peter was smarter than he pretended to be. Even the ski boots fitted okay.

I went back to the window and sat there fully

dressed except for the anorak and boots, which I left on the end of the bed. Helena might arrive any minute, and I wanted to be ready.

Outside, nothing had changed. The snow was still as thick on the ground, and judging by the dark clouds rolling down from the mountains, more would be falling soon. I hoped Helena had taken snowstorms into account when she was organising our escape.

Then I had an awful thought: what if Helena assumed I could ski, and that skiing down the mountain was to be our means of escape? I'd never even seen snow before yesterday, let alone skied on it.

Helena didn't turn up that morning, and I was deeply disappointed when the door opened at lunchtime to reveal only Peter and another tray of food. He spent some time checking the fit of the clothes. I tried not to fidget, but I was desperate for him to go so that I could see if there was any further news folded in the serviette. The moment the door closed behind him, I leapt for the table.

I whipped the serviette from the tray and shook it hard. Nothing fell out. Desperately, I inspected the hems of the serviette in the hope that a slip of paper had become lodged in one of them. There was nothing.

I finished lunch, Peter collected the tray, and it began to snow. Time stopped. The food had made me sleepy, so I lay down for a snooze.

Someone had stuffed me into a bag full of grass. I woke up with a start. It was dark. I'd been dreaming, and the itching of my skin was driving me mad. I jumped up, ripped the woollen clothes off, gave myself a hard rub down with a towel, then got dressed again with my cotton pyjamas underneath.

It was snowing heavily. The air outside my window, lit by the light from my room, was thick with snowflakes. I wondered again about Helena's plans: did they include darkness, as well as skiing and snowstorms?

I was bored. I had never been so bored in my whole life. My boredom was even stronger than my fear.

It's not that I wasn't afraid. I was. A screwed-up knotted feeling was sitting in the pit of my stomach the whole time. But having nothing to do was wearing me down even more than the fear.

I spent a lot of time studying the Domerian newspaper. I must have gone through it twenty or thirty times. I even invented rules for myself, like only being allowed to look at advertisements, or only trying to pronounce the names of women in the photographs. I tried to match the Domerian names with things in the photos. For example, there was a picture of some people on a ski-slope and I recognised the word 'ski' on a banner in the background.

There were cartoons as well, but they didn't make me laugh. I spent a long time on the crossword, trying to fill it in with English words, which was a challenge without a pencil.

I searched hardest for the Prime Minister who was responsible for keeping me in prison, and I reckon I narrowed it down to two men in a photo of some politicians in a parliament. I thought one of the men might even have been Leo's dad, but neither of them looked like Leo, so I couldn't decide.

The newspaper did distract me, but there were times when I stared at its pages without seeing a single thing. At those times my thoughts were a long way away, with Mum, Dad and Henry.

The falling snow was now lit by floodlights, but the mountains had disappeared. I'd folded up the newspaper and had been watching the snow fall for a long time when I heard the sound of keys again.

I couldn't believe how pleased I was to see Peter. A swell of pleasure rose in my chest, but I forced myself to stay by the window, as cool as I could. But although I was pleased to see him, I was also desperate for him to go. I had to check the serviette.

I waited and waited, but he wouldn't leave. First, he looked into the bathroom, then went out to the corridor and fetched two new rolls of toilet paper, two clean towels, and two bars of soap. Then he went back out to the corridor and came back with a duster, and started dusting the table, the bedside cabinet, the doorframes, and the window ledge next to where I was sitting.

I didn't move, but inside I was screaming, 'Why do you have to do housework now!?'

Finally, he ran out of things to dust, and left.

I leapt off my chair, tripped over, rolled, and was up and at the table without missing a beat. I grabbed the serviette, shook it out. Nothing! I pulled everything off the tray. But still there was nothing.

15

Thursday night

I slumped down at the table. I let my head sink onto it. I could hardly bring myself to look at the food, let alone eat it. Helena had said we were going to escape, but what I needed was confirmation of her promise, because I was starting to believe I'd just dreamed the whole thing.

I picked at the food. My appetite was gone, but I forced myself to eat by telling myself that this meal was *definitely* the last I would be having in prison. Brown stew with potatoes, green beans, yellow corn, orange carrots, black bread, white wine, and white yoghurt. At least the food was colourful.

I nibbled my way through it, then went back to watching the snow fall. It was coming down more heavily now, and even the sheds were nearly invisible. The world was closing in on me.

Peter came for the tray. I didn't even look at him. I told myself I was conserving energy for the escape by not turning my head. But the truth was that I was teetering on the verge of howling, and I was afraid that even a glance at him would tip me over the edge. I'd never felt so black and empty.

I didn't want to move, but after a while, I forced myself to get up and walk around. I did one circuit of the room, running my hand along the wall, then a half circuit that brought me back to the table again. I looked at it in surprise. There, in the middle of it, was a small plastic bag.

Peter must have left it when he collected my dinner tray. I approached it with caution, peeling open the top as if expecting something to leap out. Inside were several little boxes. It took me a moment to work out what they were: snacks in packets—nuts, muesli bars, dried fruit, and even fruit juice.

Why had Peter left them for me? Could he have meant them as comfort food to help me through the night? If he had, it was such a kind thing to do that I almost cried, but I forced myself not to. Then I came up with a more obvious explanation: Peter was just trying to prevent me from demanding more food by smashing the door again. I closed the bag, and pushed it into one of the anorak pockets. I would use it as my emergency stash for the escape.

I returned to my window chair. Again.

The vehicles were now snow-covered lumps. At the rate it was snowing, even the building I was in would soon be covered. What if I had to sit at this window until the snow melted in spring?

I must have fallen asleep with my head resting against the glass, because when the rattle of keys woke me, my right ear was freezing. My first panicked thought was that the Smart Man had come back to question me. Still dazed from sleep, I decided then and there that I would tell him anything he wanted to hear, just as long as he'd send me straight back to England.

But it was Peter.

He had a pair of white ski boots in one hand.

'Come on,' he said. 'Put on your coat, carry your boots, leave the suitcase, but bring the bag of food. Please keep quiet.'

I thought my frozen ear was playing tricks on me. I stood up and stared at him.

'You speak English,' I said.

'Yes,' he hissed. 'Hurry up!'

What was going on? Was I being taken away for questioning? My throat went dry. Suddenly, fear was stronger than boredom. I tried to push the word 'interrogation' out of my head, but it wouldn't go away.

But why was Peter whispering? He was the guard, I was the prisoner. Was he worried about waking the other prisoners?

I pulled on the anorak and picked up the ski boots while he stood in the doorway, looking up and down the corridor. As soon as I was ready, he beckoned to me, and we went out together. I noticed that he hadn't handcuffed me, and wasn't pushing me along roughly as I might have expected.

The corridor was long and wide. It had white walls and a polished wooden floor. Along one side there were windows looking out into the night, and on the other were doors with padlocks on them, just like mine. More corridors went off to the left.

We reached a corner. Peter signalled for me to stop, and while I stood flat against the wall, he crept forward and listened. Then he signalled me to follow again.

I was confused. It didn't look like he was taking me for interrogation, but could I really believe that we were escaping? My heart was racing, but I forced myself to breathe as calmly as possible.

We made a cautious right turn into a short corridor at the end of which was a lift foyer. Peter signalled me to stop again, and went forward to put his ear against the metal doors of the lifts. He shook his head, and waved for me to follow him through a fire door beside the lifts.

We started down the concrete stairs, passing doors on every second landing. Peter went ahead and listened at each door before waving me past. We descended four or five floors.

I was perplexed. After hours of sitting at the barred window I had figured that my prison room was on the second floor. By my calculations we were now at least two or three floors underground. Thoughts of dungeons and underground torture chambers flashed into my mind. But Peter's behaviour simply did not match.

Suddenly he stopped. At first I couldn't work out what the problem was. Then I heard footsteps on the stairs below. Peter looked around quickly for somewhere to hide. There was nowhere, just wide grey stairs with white walls. There wasn't even the smallest gap for me to squeeze into.

Peter bent down and quickly put on his left ski boot, snapping the clips closed. Then he grabbed me by the shoulders, dragged me to the nearest landing and shoved me into a corner. Holding his right boot in front of him he leaned back against me until my nose was buried in the back of his coat.

The footsteps came closer.

Peter must have been fiddling with the boot in front of him because I could feel his arms moving. The footsteps arrived on our landing and stopped. The Smart Man said something in Domerian. When Peter replied, I felt his voice vibrating through his coat. His arms moved some more. I think he was showing the other man his boot. The Smart Man said something else, laughed, and then the footsteps started climbing again. Peter laughed too, and shouted something. Then gradually the pressure eased off my nose.

He didn't say a word as he stepped forward to let me out of the corner. He put his other boot on and we kept going down the stairs.

By the time we got to the door at the bottom, I was sure we were a long way underground. But I was wrong. Peter listened at the door, then slowly pushed it open. Beyond was a long corridor with glass walls and a glass roof. The roof was covered with snow. Then I understood. As well as descending the fire stairs inside the building, we had also been climbing down the slope of the mountain on which it was built.

The tunnel must have been at least a hundred metres long, and if it hadn't been for the snow, we would have been as visible as mice in a perspex cage.

At the far end we pushed through a set of double doors into a huge brightly-lit shed. I was delighted to see a cable car sitting on tracks between two platforms with guardrails, and with a pair of thick steel cables attached to its roof. I wasn't going to have to ski, after all!

Peter hurried me along the side of the shed to a room filled with brooms and shovels and big bins.

'Wait here. I will return,' he whispered. 'Hide yourself. Put your boots on.'

'What's happening?' I asked.

'Later,' he said, and went away.

I tucked myself in behind one of the bins, fine-tuning my ears to every sound.

One thing was worrying me. Where was the Smart Man headed when we met him on the stairs? If he was on his way to interrogate me, then he would have discovered I was gone by now, and raised the alarm. Or, if he was on his way to question Helena, then maybe she would be delayed, and our escape put in jeopardy.

Peter was so long in returning that I'd begun to make alternative plans for a solo escape, perhaps by toboggan, or by hijacking the cable car by myself. But then the door opened.

I didn't move. What if it wasn't Peter? It could have been the Smart Man.

Then a woman whispered my name. It was the voice I had been waiting to hear. But even though I knew it was Helena, I stayed where I was in case the Smart Man was holding her hostage.

'Isabella,' she whispered again.

I still didn't move.

'Isabella?' Peter called quietly. Then I heard him say, 'I told her to wait here. I didn't think she would wander off.'

I decided to chance it. We had to move quickly in case the alarm had been raised. I slipped out from behind the bin, and was relieved to see just Peter and Helena standing there.

'I'm so pleased to see you!' I cried.

'Oh, Isabella. What terrible trouble we have caused you.'

'You can talk later,' Peter whispered. 'We must go now.'

We followed him out of the storeroom, but instead of going to the cable car, he headed towards the far end of the shed. We passed eight doors, each with Domerian words stencilled on them, but when Peter opened the last door I knew that I was in trouble. My stomach did a terrible twist as I read the only recognisable word out of the three stencilled there. *SKI*.

I had been right all along about the ski boots.

'I can't ski,' I said. 'I've never skied in my life.'

They looked at me in astonishment.

'You don't ski in Australia?' Helena asked.

'People do. My Grandma does. But I never have.'

'It doesn't matter,' Peter said, looking like it mattered a lot. 'We'll take her down the mountain between us.'

We came out of the shed holding our skis and poles. Once Helena and Peter had put their skis and helmets on, and had put me into mine, and after Helena had said 'keep your knees bent', they grabbed me by the arms and we were away.

The lights from the shed lit the first hundred metres of snow, and the hairs on my neck prickled at the thought of someone seeing us emerge onto the slope. There was no tree cover at all. The mountainside under the cable car cables was completely open. I imagined what an easy target we would make in the moonlight, silhouetted against the snow.

Within seconds we had skied over a crest and were accelerating down a steeper slope into the darkness. A wall of pine trees loomed up in front of us, and suddenly Helena and Peter were swerving me left and right between the trunks.

'Switch your helmet light on,' Helena shouted, as we plunged into an even darker dark amongst the trees. She reached up and a piercing light beamed from the front of her helmet. I found the switch on my helmet as Peter switched on his light too. The pine trees sprang out at us in the bright beams.

The forest was fairly open and, most of the time, as we raced between the trees, Peter and Helena kept a firm grip on my upper arms. But every now and again, a gap was too narrow for the three of us, and one of them would let go and fall behind. The first time Peter let go, I screamed and flung out my arm to grab him, but I stayed upright, and within seconds he was back at my side. Then they both let go, and I had to ski by myself for some terrifying seconds before they grabbed me again.

We swerved at high speed through the forest for

a long time, but at last the slope began to flatten, and the trees began to thin out.

We switched off our helmet lights and slid out across sloping moonlit fields, their fences almost buried by snow. I saw only two houses, one with a lighted window and smoke snaking from its chimney, but otherwise the landscape was empty for kilometres around.

Helena and Peter were heading towards two rows of trees in the distance. Within fifteen minutes of leaving the forest we were concealed amongst their trunks beside a road, our skis already buried in the snow behind us.

'If all is well,' Peter said. 'A car will come for us within twenty minutes.'

'It will take us somewhere safe,' said Helena, removing her ski helmet and shaking out her hair. 'Then we can arrange for you to be reunited with your father.'

I nodded mutely, dazed and soaked with sweat from our ride down the mountain. Every single nerve in my body was singing. I unbuttoned my anorak to release some heat.

'That place isn't a prison, is it?' I asked at last.

'It is not,' Helena answered. 'It is Mont Noir, the mountain campus of the National University of Domeria. I studied there for four years. You and I were held prisoner in the student halls of residence.'

'There weren't any students, though?'

'Not one. The first thing the government did, after they arrested André and Theresa, was close the university campuses. They thought to prevent protests by this action.'

I pulled out the bag of snacks I'd stashed in my anorak and gulped some juice. 'They thought they'd stop the students organising marches and stuff?' I asked.

'They did,' Helena nodded. 'But they miscalculated. The students are marching and protesting in the capital instead.'

I turned to Peter. 'And how come you were a guard up there, and now you're on our side? And why did you pretend you couldn't speak English?'

'I am a member of the security forces,' he answered, brushing snow from his hands. 'The Government took our loyalty for granted. But they were wrong to do so. Not all of us support their corrupt ways. I have been stationed at Mont Noir since André and Theresa Bruin were arrested.'

'But why didn't you tell me you were a friend?' I asked. 'It would have made things a whole heap easier for me.'

'I didn't know how you would behave under interrogation. You could have betrayed me.'

He had a point. 'How *did* I behave under interrogation, then?' I asked.

'With commendable dignity,' he answered. 'But it would not have been long before you revealed everything you knew, probably including the fact that I had spoken to you, despite my orders to keep you isolated'.

His explanation had a horrible logic to it: he couldn't afford to spare my feelings if it meant I might betray him.

'But how many prisoners were there?' I asked. 'The place felt empty to me.'

'You and Helena only,' Peter said. 'There were to be many more, but the cable car broke down, and the other prisoners could not be persuaded to ski uphill to captivity.'

'Bad timing,' I said.

'No, no, perfect timing.' Peter laughed again. 'I arranged it myself.'

Helena looked surprised. '*You* arranged it!'

'And what about the smart man who asked me all the questions I couldn't answer? Who was he?'

'Egon Ray. He is loyal to the government. He was expecting to build an empire of political prisoners on Mont Noir. That is, until I sabotaged the cable car.'

'Is Egon Ray going to have us chased?' I asked. It had suddenly occurred to me that we were getting away very casually.

'The most he could have done was make a

phone call to the police,' said Peter. 'But I took his mobile phone and cut the phone lines.'

'But he took *my* mobile!' Helena said.

'In that case,' Peter said, 'I may have miscalculated . . . Where is that damned car?'

We were in a black Mercedes, driving fast, sliding along a snow-covered road. I was holding tight in the back with Helena, while Peter was braced in the front beside Saul, the driver.

We had driven in silence for some time before I felt brave enough to ask if anyone knew anything about Leo. 'Is Leo safe?' I asked Saul.

'Leo is here?' Helena asked, obviously surprised.

'He came in Dad's cousin's truck a couple of nights ago,' I told her.

'Leo is at headquarters,' said Saul.

'The emergency headquarters for the Domerian Democratic Party,' Peter explained. 'We are headed there now.'

Saul corrected a skid that had my side of the car within centimetres of a fence-post. I edged towards the centre of the back seat. 'Can I phone Dad from there?' I asked.

'Perhaps we can get a line to England,' Saul answered.

'To *England*?' I asked. I had been assuming that Dad would be in Domeria trying to rescue me.

'Your father was at Domeria City Airport very briefly,' Saul said. 'But he was deported on the next flight.'

Dad suddenly felt impossibly far away—and yet he'd been so close. 'I'd really like to call him,' I said.

'We'll try to arrange it,' said Saul, flipping the wheel to correct a slide. He had no room for error between the road and the tree-lined verges.

I felt so despondent about Dad, and so alarmed by Saul's driving, that I was desperate to distract myself. 'So how did I get up to the university then?' I asked. 'I know I didn't ski uphill . . . and also, why was I kidnapped at all?'

'I believe Erik Booré's team were scared to come back empty-handed,' Peter answered. 'They knew you and your father had helped Leo. They certainly thought your involvement was more organised than it actually was.'

'Which is why Egon Ray kept talking about our organisation.'

'That man has the strangest ideas!' Helena said quietly.

'He is a fool,' Peter agreed. 'And because he is a fool, he has risen through the ranks. He was on his way to question you again when he passed us on the stairs. He would have woken you up, and found you all the more vulnerable because of that.'

'I was feeling pretty edgy,' I agreed, feeling

edgier still as we slid broadside around a corner.

'But to answer your other question,' Peter continued, unfazed by the crazy drive. 'You and Helena were transported to the campus by helicopter.'

'And I slept through it!'

Holding tight to her door, Helena turned to me. 'But Isabella, you have not yet told me how you came to be so caught up in our affairs. Leo involved you of course.'

The wild ride continued as I repeated the story, beginning with Leo's call to us at Copthorne.

'But three journeys to Stone Cross!' Helena exclaimed when I'd finished. 'And that fearful factory! And your family . . .' She shook her head and turned away to look out of the window, clearly unsettled.

'Did they use that sleeping stuff on you?' I asked. 'They did on me. Twice.'

'Sleeping stuff?' she mumbled, her face averted. 'No, no.'

We pulled onto a road that had been cleared of snow, and for the first time Saul was able to drive in a straight line.

'There was one thing we all wondered about,' I said. 'Did you use your credit card at the hotel?'

'I don't think so,' Helena said, turning back to me. 'Why do you ask?'

'That might be how they traced you and Leo.'

'Perhaps I did, then.' She frowned as she thought back. 'I might have done. I can't remember. Perhaps they simply followed us!'

I suddenly noticed a throbbing sound. 'What's that?' I asked.

Peter opened his window and listened.

'Helicopter,' he said. 'Sounds like an EC 145.'

Saul immediately reached forward to switch off the headlights, but we continued to speed along the moonlit road.

In a matter of moments the approaching helicopter was making the car vibrate. A few seconds later it was as though a giant mallet was thumping on the car. The noise was deafening. I thought the car was going to shake apart. Saul wrenched the steering wheel, and the car skidded and slid to a stop. I was thrown against Helena, who was thrown hard against her door. The noise hammered on.

'Where is it?' I screamed.

Then a beam of light, a pillar of blinding white, suddenly burned down onto the ground not more than twenty metres from us. It was so bright I expected the ground to burst into flames.

'Run,' Saul shouted, as the pillar of light crept towards us.

I reached out, found the door handle in the dark, and pushed the door wide. I launched myself into the snow and scrambled for a tree. I couldn't see anything but the blinding light that was stalking us. I scrabbled at the snow, trying to bury myself.

Then suddenly the light tilted aside, swerved and twisted away. I watched as it lit up a wall of trees beyond me, touched the tree tops, and suddenly went out, plunging everything into darkness.

The clattering of the helicopter receded. I scrambled back to the car to rejoin the others, and we watched as the helicopter, glinting in the moonlight, flew towards Mont Noir.

As we climbed into the Mercedes, something strange occurred to me.

'If Egon Ray can phone for a helicopter,' I said, 'how come he can't phone for twenty police cars?'

'Good question, Isabella,' said Peter.

Helena just shrugged.

16

Friday

The rest of the ninety-minute drive was uneventful.
That is, until a man pulled us over as we were
turning into a track that led off the road.

I didn't notice anything at first, but then the
man shifted a rifle from his shoulder into his hands.

'Gun,' I warned.

'Friend,' said Peter, as Saul rolled his window
down. The gunman raised a hand in greeting, and
after a brief conversation in Domerian, opened the
gate that blocked the track.

Our Mercedes started to climb up through the
pine forest, and Helena and I were thrown about,
despite our seatbelts, as Saul wrestled the car over
the rough terrain. The track was narrow, not more
than a single lane, and in some places there was
barely enough room for the Mercedes to squeeze
between the trees. We were climbing for over an
hour, brushing through pine branches, fording
creeks, crawling up steep slopes with our tyres
spinning in mud and patches of snow. We passed

through two more gates guarded by armed men.

Just as I thought I couldn't stand one more minute of jolting, we crawled out of the forest onto a wide gravel drive. A dark stone house with crumbling towers loomed a few hundred metres away in the centre of the clearing. The sun was just rising, glittering on the three mountaintops in the distance. If it hadn't been for the car we were travelling in, I could have believed myself transported into a fairytale.

Leo must have been warned of our arrival. As we pulled up, he burst out of the front doors of the house and came flying down the steps.

'Isabella!' he shouted. 'You are safe. Thank God, you are safe.' He flung my door open before Saul had even cut the ignition.

If this was my chance to play it cool, I missed the chance completely. Before I knew it, I was out of the car giving Leo a crushing hug.

The entrance hall of the dark stone house was vast. Even Peter was dwarfed by it. It was bigger than the whole downstairs of our house in Sydney, and had an enormous chandelier like a colossal cartwheel suspended over the centre of it. The floor was made of stones fitted into each other like a jigsaw puzzle, and stretched out to the foot of a wide timber staircase. The stairs climbed up to a landing under a tall window made of small panes of glass, and the walls of the hall were constructed of stones so large that I couldn't begin to imagine how many people it would have taken to lift them.

Even though it was only eight in the morning, and barely light outside, the foyer was busy. I had already counted seven different people crossing the floor. Leo was beside me, talking quietly to a short-haired woman with a notebook, but Helena, Peter and Saul had disappeared.

While Leo continued his discussion, I wandered across to a pair of double doors on the left side of the hall. What I saw surprised me. Unlike the ancient entrance hall, the room beyond was bright and clean, with smooth walls, modern desks, telephones and computers.

'This is a new addition,' Leo said from behind me. 'The rest of this house was built over three hundred years ago.'

White people have only been in Australia for *two* hundred, I thought.

'Domeria was at war with itself at that time. My ancestor, Hector Bruin, built it as a place of refuge.'

'What a shame that you need to use it as a refuge again,' I said.

'Our real home, Bruin House, is also built of this mountain stone,' Leo continued. 'But it is an elegant structure, with fine turrets and grand rooms. It stands only thirty kilometres from here, to the northwest. We hope to live there again one day.'

'This is pretty grand, though,' I said cheerfully.

'I suppose it is. We have made it habitable. But in better times, you will see our beautiful Bruin House. As well as being our home, it is also the home of the Domerian Democratic Party.'

'When your father's not in prison,' I said without thinking, then wished I hadn't.

Leo nodded, the brightness gone from his eyes.

Peter came into the hall on his way to the office. 'Isabella, I have arranged for you to talk to your father,' he said. 'It is necessary to arrange a secure line, so that the call is not traced back to here. Perhaps within two hours, maybe a little more, you may speak to your father for a few minutes.'

'Thankyou so much,' I said, and Peter excused himself. The excitement of arriving at the house had made me forget Dad for a while, but now my need to hear his voice came rushing back.

'Have you still got my mobile?' I asked Leo.

'Yes, of course,' he said, reaching into his pocket. 'But it's no use to you here. There is no reception within thirty kilometres. We use a satellite system for our communications.'

I nodded. I wouldn't have used it at the house anyway, since I knew mobiles were traceable.

'Here's Karen,' said Leo, as a tall blonde woman about Mum's age emerged from a doorway from the back of the hall. 'Karen is our housekeeper. Karen, I would like you to meet the courageous Isabella. Would you show her to her room? I have some messages to send.'

Leo headed for the office and we climbed the stairs to the first floor, where there was a sitting area with armchairs and coffee tables, and two long corridors leading off to the left and right.

'This will be your room,' Karen said, opening the third door along the left-hand corridor. 'I think you will be comfortable.'

She crossed to the windows and pulled back the curtains. Pale light leaked in through the leadlight windows. The bedroom was big, probably half the size of the entrance hall downstairs but, unlike the foyer, it had rough plaster walls, and the stone showed through only where sections of plaster had fallen off. There was a large wardrobe, a desk and a dressing table, as well as the wide wooden bed. A leather couch, a coffee table and two armchairs filled the remaining space.

'I have found some fresh clothes for you,' Karen said, smiling at the shirt and knickerbockers I was wearing. 'The bathroom is at the end of the hall, and there is a phone on your bedside table if you require anything else. Please do not hesitate to call for anything at all.'

She left, and I dragged off my ski boots and

socks, the clothes and my pyjamas, slipped into the dressing gown that Karen had left and I went along the corridor to the bathroom.

The steaming hot shower was fantastic. Feeling almost awake after yet another sleepless night, I went back to my room and dressed in the underclothes, black jeans, tee shirt and black jumper. Then I lay down, just to be comfortable, until they were ready for me to talk to Dad.

The phone on my bedside table was ringing. I couldn't work out where I was. I picked the phone up automatically and a man said, 'Isabella?'

'Dad!' I yelled.

'Isabella, thank God,' said Dad.

'It's so good to hear you, Dad,' I said, making a huge effort not to cry. 'Where are you?'

'I'm at Aunty Jane's place. I've tried so hard to get to you, Isabella. I was positive they'd taken you to Domeria. You know, a noise woke me up. I checked around the house, then I came to check on you and you were gone. I woke everyone up. We searched the house and the garden and everywhere. Gary and Alice were all for going to the police, but I took the first plane to Domeria. Believe it or not, they had my name on a database at the airport, and sent me straight home again. Then I flew to this place called Belleau, but I couldn't find a way of getting into

Domeria. It was hopeless, so I climbed on a plane back home. But how are you, baby?'

'I'm all right, Dad. I'm being looked after. I'm safe here.'

'Thank God. I've told Mum you're safe now. She sends her love. I love you too.'

I started to cry. Then a woman's voice came on the line. 'I'm sorry, but we must cut the connection.'

And Dad was gone.

I didn't get to tell him I loved him. The relief I'd felt at hearing his voice was gone and I wailed like an animal.

There was a knock on the door. I rubbed my eyes to make sure there was no sign of tears. 'Come in,' I said.

It was Helena and Leo—but not the Leo I'd known that morning.

'My God, what's happened to you?' I shouted.

'It is a disguise,' Leo said, blushing, and touching his hair with his hand.

Leo's dark hair was now short and spiky blond, and he had acquired a goatee beard.

'Would you have recognised him in the street?' Helena asked.

I shook my head.

'Don't laugh at me,' Leo said. 'It is bad enough that I give myself a shock every time I walk past a mirror.'

I laughed anyway. 'It looks so cool,' I said, and he blushed again.

There was another knock, and Karen came in. 'Is Isabella ready?' she said.

'Ready for what?' I asked.

'Your face is known now by many people,' said Helena. 'As we move through the country there will be military checkpoints through which we must pass. Your identity will be checked. For added safety, we would like to change your appearance, too.'

'I'm not wearing a beard,' I said.

'No beard,' said Karen, smiling, 'but we want to make your hair and eyebrows blonde.'

I nodded. I was prepared to do anything that would get me home safe to Dad.

Karen and I went back to the bathroom. It didn't take long. My scalp and forehead tingled, my nostrils filled with the stink of chemicals she was using, and inside an hour I was staring at someone in the mirror that I didn't quite recognise.

My hair and eyebrows were blonde instead of dark brown, and the change in colour made my skin look more tanned.

After a sandwich in the kitchen and a chat with the chef, I dropped by the office to show off my new disguise to Leo, Helena and Peter. When they'd recovered from their surprise, Leo introduced me to Patrice, a bald man with glasses; Otto, a tall grey-haired man; and two strong-looking blonde women, Jeanne and Marie. When Leo described me as his saviour, they applauded, and it was my turn to blush.

While Leo got me a chair, Peter sorted through some papers, and pulled out a sheet of handwritten notes. We listened as he explained what had been decided about my immediate future.

'You'll go tonight after dark,' he began. 'The checkpoint guards change at midnight, and we like to travel near the end of their shifts, as we think they are more tired and consequently less diligent at that time. Saul will drive you into the northern part of the Lodo Mountains. Depending on the location of the government checkpoints—they move them some-times—there are two places where you can be taken across the border. Saul will make a judgement as to which to use. Whichever crossing he chooses, someone will meet you on the other side.'

'That sounds good,' I said. 'But what happens across the border?'

'You will be taken to an airport and put on a commercial flight back to England,' Peter explained.

'But my passport's at Copthorne,' I said. 'I'll need a passport to fly to England.'

'Travel documents in a false identity will be provided,' said Peter.

'It's a long wait, but there are English-language books in the other office,' Helena said.

'You may walk in the grounds, but do not go far from the house,' added Peter. 'The perimeter guards will not allow you to enter the forest.'

'Wild animals?' I asked.

'Perhaps of the government kind,' said Leo. 'But there are some wolves too, in the remoter parts.'

'If you'll excuse us, Isabella,' Peter said, tapping his papers into shape. 'Helena and I must prepare for a strategy meeting.'

I took the hint.

'What are you doing?' I asked Leo.

'Nothing for one hour. We can walk if you like.'

Leo and I put on sheepskin coats from a rack by the front doors, and went down the steps to the driveway. The weather had turned greyer and colder, and I buttoned the collar around my ears.

The driveway ran across the clearing and disappeared into the solid wall of pine trees out of which we'd driven that morning. Two guards were just visible at the edge of the forest.

'We skied through a forest like that coming down Mont Noir,' I said.

'Peter told me you hadn't skied before.'

'They were both *really* shocked.'

'Skiing is second nature to Domerians. Just like swimming is for many Australians. Come this way.'

We walked along the front of the house under the tall windows, then turned along the side of it. A pile of stones blocked our way. I looked up to see the crooked remains of a tower.

'The house is falling down,' Leo said.

We skirted the rubble and continued our walk while Leo told me in detail about his race across Europe in Derek's truck. It had taken a night, a day, and part of another night of hard driving east along freeways through France, Germany and Austria, then onto smaller roads through the Czech Republic and Slovakia.

'It had been dark for a while by the time we got to Domeria. I guided Derek to a place within five kilometres of where I could cross the frontier.'

'Five kilometres,' I repeated, as we climbed through a fence into a yard of derelict sheds at the rear of the house. 'That's a long way to walk in the middle of the night.'

'His truck would have been too conspicuous on the border roads. But I was at the border by two.'

'You must have been dead on your feet.'

'I was so happy to be home that tiredness was not an issue,' he said. 'Although I still had a long way to go before I found refuge with friends.'

We walked on.

'Mont Bruin,' Leo said, pointing to a snow-capped mountain in the distance. 'It was named for my family eight hundred years ago. Perhaps now you can understand why I yearned to return home.

Bruin House stands beneath it.'

I tried to imagine what it would be like to have a mountain named after your family, or what it would be like to belong to a place for eight hundred years. It didn't work. Mum and Dad had only been in our house for twenty years.

'What are you going to do when all this is over?' I asked.

'Study Political Science at Mont Noir University.'

'And be the Prime Minister, I bet.'

'Only if the people wish for it to be so,' he said. 'That is the whole point. We may become leaders, but we are also the servants of the people we lead.'

We wandered along a path lined with rose-bushes. A garden bench at the end gave a perfect view of Mont Bruin. We sat and chatted, and watched dark clouds gathering around its summit, and lost track of time until Leo suddenly jumped up looking at his watch.

'The strategy meeting with Peter, Patrice and Helena. We have to plan what to do next. I'll see you afterwards.'

'You mean you *don't know*?' I muttered to myself as Leo disappeared around the corner of the house.

I wandered the grounds for another hour, then went inside, where Karen took me to a small sitting room. We sat beside the stove and she told me about Domeria, while I answered her questions about Australia. I knew she was trying to help me pass the time before my departure, but after we'd exhausted what I knew about Australia, she left to do some housekeeping.

In the silence I started to worry about all the government checkpoints that were between me and freedom. The guards with rifles: rifles that might mean death for me if they found out who I was. At the very least, those guards would clap me back in prison—real prison this time, not a comfy room at Mont Noir. How would Peter get me out then? How would Dad find me?

I jumped up. If I sat alone in that room any longer, worrying about the future, I'd go mad. I needed a distraction. It was too cold and dark to go outside again, so I set off to explore the house.

I climbed to the first floor and headed past my bedroom along the corridor, peering through doors as I went. The first rooms I looked into were almost habitable, with drooping wallpaper and sagging ceilings. But after that, things became progressively worse. The very last room was missing half of its floor, had no windows, and a whole corner of the room had fallen out.

The other side of the house was virtually the same. Except for one thing. I was wandering along the corridor, and starting to lose interest, when I thought I heard voices. I walked on more slowly,

168

Eleven Days

following the sound. As I got nearer to the end of the corridor the voices grew louder. Then I saw a thin band of light under the last door.

I stopped outside, listening to the rumbling voices. They were so muffled that I could barely tell whether or not it was Domerian they were speaking. I had just decided to stop eavesdropping when Leo's voice was raised above the rest.

'... ... ... Isabella ... ... Mont Noir!' he shouted angrily in Domerian.

As soon as I heard my name, I put my ear to the door.

'Jane ... Alice ... Gary ... ... Stone Cross ... ' Leo sounded angrier still.

'But the *English* girl and her *English* family did *not* rescue me!' Helena shouted in English, and I couldn't believe my burning ear.

'She is *Australian*!' Leo roared back.

Then I heard Peter and another man's voice trying to calm them.

But Helena took no notice. 'Of course I'm grateful to those English,' she snapped, sounding anything but grateful.

I waited for Leo to correct her, but he didn't.

'All I'm saying, Leo, is that it's a good thing she is leaving tonight. It is time for the professionals to do their work. Amateur hour is over!'

17

Friday Night

I was fuming. I was steaming. I couldn't believe my ear hadn't burst into flames. And I certainly couldn't believe the words coming out of Helena's mouth. Piccadilly Circus, Stone Cross, the black factory, me being snatched from Copthorne. Didn't that count for anything?

I'd grabbed the door handle and was in the room before I knew what I was doing. The five people around the table were as startled as I was by my surprise arrival.

'Isabella?' Leo said, standing up.

'I heard talking,' I mumbled lamely, my anger momentarily forgotten

'Can we help you?' Patrice asked.

I didn't want to tell them that I'd been eaves-dropping, or that I had heard what Helena had said. But I did need an excuse for being there.

'I was wandering . . . Wondering whether the meeting was over yet . . . I was sitting alone, down-stairs and worrying. I know everyone's busy . . . but

. . . but . . . can I be part of this meeting?'

They looked even more surprised. Then Patrice laughed. 'Oh I don't think so, young lady.'

'Why not, Patrice?' Leo said. 'If risking her life for the freedom of Domeria is not sufficient qualification to sit at this table, what is?'

'It is only a planning meeting, Isabella,' Patrice continued, ignoring Leo. 'Boring business. You would not be interested.'

My anger was building, but I held my voice calm. 'I was interested enough to rescue Leo,' I said.

Otto nodded. 'She has a point, Patrice.'

'She has a right to be here,' Leo said. 'I vote that Isabella be allowed to join us.' He raised his hand.

Peter and Otto raised their hands too. Helena's hand followed more reluctantly. Patrice's hand stayed where it was on the table.

When I first sat down, I thought that, at best, it would be fascinating to hear these professionals organise the downfall of the government. At worst, I thought, it would fill in some more hours before my escape. But it seemed that the only item on the agenda was the need to formulate a plan to spring André and Theresa Bruin from prison.

'Only they can pull the party together and stir people into action,' Peter told me.

'Leo and I have been completely out of touch with events since his father and mother were arrested,' explained Helena. 'Many of the other senior people in the party have also been arrested. The party organisation has been badly disrupted.'

These explanations were delivered to me in English, but Patrice, who was the security chief of the Domerian Democratic Party, continued to speak in Domerian. Leo translated for a while, but then asked for another vote. By a majority of four to one, English was made the rule of the meeting.

Patrice glowered. 'Perhaps if we speak in English someone might actually think of a plan,' he sneered.

'What have you come up with so far?' I asked in an attempt to melt the ice out of the air.

Leo shook his head. 'Nothing yet.'

'It does not please me to say this,' said Patrice, 'but in the absence of any better ideas, if we are to resolve this crisis I think we will have to adopt the tactics of our enemies. I say this for two reasons. First, the longer the crisis is allowed to continue, the more control the government will exert. They will probably use the army to clear the streets by the end of this week at the latest. They will also close down all the media that do not support them. Consequently, everything but government inform-ation will cease to flow. With that sort of control, the government will become unassailable, and André and Theresa will be even further from freedom.'

There was a reluctant murmur of agreement with Patrice's analysis.

'And who knows how long it would take for the rest of us to be rounded up?' Patrice went on. 'No matter how many places we find to hide, slowly and surely we will all lose our freedom. And the more often we have to move, the less time we will have to organise resistance. It is for these reasons that we must act swiftly and decisively. So what I am suggesting is that we kidnap the Prime Minister.'

Peter slapped the table. 'What are you saying?' he bellowed. 'We would be no better than them!'

'Must principle always be the first casualty?' Leo shouted. 'What would my father say?'

Patrice tried to defend himself. 'I know, I know, it is not what we would wish but . . .'

Helena stared silently down at her hands.

'It would be impossible anyway,' Otto said. 'Our resources are no match for theirs. We need to be much cleverer than them. Unexpectedly clever.'

'But does anyone have a better suggestion?' Patrice snapped.

'As Patrice pointed out, we need to act swiftly,' Leo muttered.

'But we must not use their methods,' Peter said.

'So what is their greatest weakness?' Leo asked.

'The greatest weakness this government has,' said Patrice, 'is the money-laundering arrangements they are putting in place. The deals they are making are with criminal and corrupt people, and these people will eventually double-cross them.'

'The campaign of lies against André and Theresa is another thing,' Peter added. 'If we can only turn that campaign back on them somehow . . . reveal the truth . . .' He shrugged. 'But the money laundering is what will bring them down, if anything will.'

'When the government brings illegal money into your country,' I piped up, 'it will be guilty of helping criminals and terrorists, won't it?'

Patrice rolled his eyes.

'And Leo's dad was trying to stop that money coming in,' I continued.

'And he was getting close to success,' Peter said, 'until he was arrested.'

'The international community was waking up to what was happening,' Otto added.

'But they've gone to sleep again?' I asked.

'André was the driving force behind the moves against the government,' Otto explained. 'He had a high profile in Europe. But without him . . .'

'Other European leaders know Leo's dad's been shoved into prison, don't they?' I asked. 'They know this country's still doing wrong. So why aren't they doing something?'

'It is complicated.' Peter hesitated. 'Historically,

sorting out another country's internal problems has often been an excuse for invading it and stealing its assets. A situation that must be avoided. History has also proved that becoming involved in another country's problems, even with the best of intentions, usually brings trouble.'

'Dad and me got involved in a country that wasn't ours.'

Leo laughed. 'You flew into our troubles by accident.'

The others smiled, except for Patrice, who grimaced. 'We are being diverted from our purpose,' he said. 'The point of this meeting is to release André and Theresa from prison, not the political education of this young woman!'

I was starting to dislike Patrice.

The clock ticked in the silence that followed. I wondered how many more ticks there would be before I could leave for home.

'The bottom line is,' I said, just to get it clear, 'that Leo's dad has to be out of prison to stop the money laundering, right?'

'It is the only hope we have,' said Leo.

'I can't see any alternative to Patrice's idea,' said Otto. 'We kidnap the Prime Minister and exchange him for André.'

'But it does make us the same,' Helena muttered, repeating Peter's earlier sentiment.

'We exchange prisoners, and then what?' asked Peter.

'More chaos, more arrests,' said Leo.

'Whatever happens, it will end in a fight,' Patrice said.

'And Domeria will be at war with itself again,' said Peter.

'Civil war,' murmured Leo. 'That most uncivilised of things.'

'It doesn't always have to end up in war,' I said. 'Leo and I talked on the plane about Gandhi. Gandhi got the British out of India without fighting.'

Patrice dismissed my comment with a wave of his hand.

'Circumstances were different in India. The British were an outside force,' said Helena. 'But thank you, Isabella. It is important we keep our minds open.'

I looked around at the frustrated faces at the table. What a stupid world it was where people were imprisoned for doing the right thing, and others were free, even though they were doing wrong. Couldn't things be less stupid? It was then that I noticed the tiniest seed of an idea pushing up through the Australian soil of my brain.

'Can you phone the United Nations and get them to help?' I asked. 'They're like a world police-man.'

'We have spoken to their ambassador,' said Peter. 'But they are very busy in other parts of the world.'

'Could we pretend to be the United Nations?' I asked.

They stared at me as if I'd sprouted horns.

'Pretend to be the United Nations?' Helena asked. 'Whatever for?'

'To tell the government off, and insist on having Leo's dad released.'

'Silliness,' said Patrice.

'Okay, then,' I said, taking a moment to put my thoughts in order. 'On the plane from Bali, Leo told me that your Finance Minister—'

'Johann Feld,' Leo said.

'—that Johann Feld had been meeting criminals in connection with this money-laundering business.'

'This is simply repetition of what we know!' Patrice muttered.

Otto ignored him. 'That is correct,' he said. 'He and his colleagues have met people in Paris, Rome and Frankfurt. Basically, he was getting promises from criminal groups who would benefit from the new money-laundering laws.'

I wanted to get the facts absolutely perfect in my mind. 'Johann was organising bribes to allow other people's dirty money to be washed clean in Domeria?' I asked. Peter, Otto and Leo nodded. 'And we definitely couldn't pretend to be the United Nations?' I asked, again.

Patrice groaned and rolled his eyes.

'And Johann Feld is meeting criminal gang leaders overseas to arrange these bribes,' I repeated.

'How many times have we said that!' said Patrice, throwing his arms up in exasperation.

'Bear with me, Patrice,' I said. 'Bribes for themselves?'

'The people of Domeria won't see any of the money,' answered Helena. 'The ministers are arranging the finances for their retirements.'

'Have they ever had meetings with criminals in England?' I asked

'Not as far as we know,' said Otto.

The focus was hard on me now. Even Patrice was watching me.

'Very interesting,' I said. My seed of an idea had grown into a seedling. 'So, if it helped to get Leo's dad out of prison, would some of you come to England?'

'André Bruin is imprisoned here in Domeria,' Patrice replied, negative as always. 'I cannot imagine why we would go to England.'

If he was trying to discourage me, it didn't work.

'But would you come to England, if it was going to help the Bruins?' I repeated patiently.

'So what is your clever plan then, Isabella?'

Patrice fired at me. 'We have to hear it before we can even begin to think about travelling anywhere.'

'I simply need to know whether you can travel to England,' I said carefully. 'If you can't travel to England at all, I won't waste any more of your time.'

Peter looked questioningly at Otto. Otto shrugged and nodded. Helena had her eyes fixed on me.

'If you don't tell me your idea,' Patrice said, 'how can I consider whether travel outside Domeria is possible?'

'Just-tell-her-whether-it-is-possible-for-some-of-us-to-go-to-England, Patrice,' Leo said slowly and deliberately. His hands were gripped tightly together on the table.

Patrice glanced at Leo in surprise. 'I would have to stay here,' he said. 'So would the office staff. But the others at this table could go. But we can agree to nothing until Isabella tells us her idea.'

'I know,' I said. 'But I've got to talk to Dad first.

18

Friday night, Saturday morning

I was on a plane again. I was going home to England, but more importantly, I was going to talk to Dad. No matter what Patrice thought of me, I was pretty sure that the freedom of the Bruins, and maybe even the future of Domeria, depended on Dad agreeing to my plan. I also knew that even if I managed to get Dad's approval, there were still a million ways my plan could go wrong.

The meeting had finished at eight pm, and as hard as they tried, and no matter how much Patrice ranted and raved, no-one else had come up with any other ideas for releasing Leo's parents from prison. Understandably, they weren't too happy that I was keeping my plan to myself.

After dinner I excused myself, saying that I needed to rest before my escape later that night. But instead of going straight upstairs, I slipped into the office next door. The lights were off, but there was enough illumination from the entrance hall, so I didn't bother searching for the light switch.

From a desk near the door I grabbed a pad of paper, a pen and a large envelope, but just as I was turning to leave, I heard a voice whispering somewhere deeper in the room. For a moment I wondered who was whispering in the dark, but then decided it was none of my business. But as I turned to leave, my arm brushed against a desk lamp and it tipped over and crashed to the floor.

'Who's there?' Helena snapped, and I heard the sound of a phone being hung up.

'Only Isabella,' I said. 'I'm sorry, I think I've broken this lamp.'

'Why are you sneaking around in the dark?' she said crossly, coming out of the shadows.

'Getting some paper.'

'I was phoning a sick friend,' Helena explained, although I hadn't thought to ask why she, too, was sneaking around in the dark.

'I'm sorry to hear that your friend is sick,' I said. 'I'm going upstairs to have a rest.'

'So what are the pen and paper for?'

'Poetry,' I lied. 'You know, writing poems.'

'Not to write down your plan, then?' she asked.

'No,' I lied again. 'Poetry.'

'I hope Domeria brings you inspiration.'

I went upstairs and locked myself in my bedroom. Keeping my plan secret was important. Half the reason was pride: to begin with, I didn't want anyone but Dad to know about it, just in case there was a major flaw that I'd missed. The other half was a conviction that the fewer people who knew the details, the safer everyone would be.

I sat at the desk in my room and, with a degree of concentration I'd never managed with school-work, wrote down every tiny detail of my plan. As I worked, I was conscious that the course of action I was proposing could mean the difference between life and death for Leo's parents.

I had just sealed the three pages of tightly written instructions into the envelope when there was a knock at the door. I slid the envelope into a drawer and unlocked the door. It was Leo.

'I'm so pleased it's you,' I said, dragging him into the room.

'It's time for you to go.'

I locked the door again and pulled him over to the desk. 'Listen carefully,' I said, opening the drawer and showing him the envelope. 'These are the details of my plan.'

Leo reached for the envelope, but I pushed his hand away.

'Don't touch it,' I said. 'No-one, not even you, should know what I've written until my dad says okay.'

'The fewer people who know a secret, the fewer

chances there are for it to be revealed,' Leo said.

'Exactly my thinking. But the moment I've talked to Dad, I'll phone you here, and you've got to open the envelope and show it to the people who were at the meeting tonight. Including Patrice.'

'I understand.'

'And if it's agreed to, it has to be organised quickly. Because the longer the plan is known, the more chance there is that the secret will leak.'

'You are thinking like a spy, Isabella.'

'But it's your parents who are in danger,' I said. 'Now take it and hide it.' I passed him the envelope. 'Don't let anyone know that you've even seen it, let alone hidden it. Not even Helena.'

'Not a single person, I promise you.' And suddenly he took my hand and kissed me on the cheek. 'But you must go now,' he said. 'Saul is waiting for you. We have phoned your father to say you are coming. Bon voyage, Isabella. Keep safe.'

I heard my name called from the stairs. Leo thrust the envelope into his shirt, unlocked the door and was gone.

By the time we had bounced down the hill through the forest and reached the open road, the clock in the dashboard of the Mercedes read 23:25.

'We are heading north-west from here,' Saul said, as we picked up speed on the sealed road. 'Our route will take us past Bruin House and around the base of Mont Bruin.'

I chattered non-stop as we drove. Saul nodded and pretended to be interested as I ran through my complete family history and an enormous amount of information about my friends, my school, Mum's carpentry skills, Dad's talents for accents, Henry's trumpet talent, Australia, Sydney, and even some of the animals I'd known. My chatter was mostly nerves, and it seemed there was nothing I could do to stop the torrent of words.

But Saul wasn't nervous. He drove calmly and quickly along the narrow roads, no straight section of which was longer than a few hundred metres before it doubled back to climb higher. As we climbed towards the base of Mont Bruin, patches of snow began to appear in the tree-lined meadows beside the road. Not long after, the trees became scarcer, the roadside verges steeper, and the whole mountainside was blanketed in snow.

Saul worked constantly at the wheel, correcting skids and slides as we sped around the corners. 'Black ice,' he said calmly, pulling the car straight after sliding sideways for ten metres on a short downhill stretch.

We were soon above the tree line.

'Look down to your right,' Saul said as we rounded a corner that had been cut from the mountain.

I looked down into a wide valley below to see a grand turreted house gleaming in the moonlight.

'Bruin House,' Saul said.

'I hope . . .' I murmured.

'We all are hoping,' said Saul.

I soon discovered that the black Mercedes was more than just a fancy car.

Almost two hours after first hitting the open road, Saul slid the Mercedes to a halt on the only wide piece of road I'd seen for an hour.

'When we descend this slope,' he said, 'there will be a checkpoint at the bottom. Maybe five Ks from here. You have to hide.'

'In the boot?' I asked doubtfully.

'No, come with me,' he said, and stepped out of the car.

I climbed out into the icy air. Saul had already opened the rear door and was lifting the seat to reveal a small space beneath it.

'In there?' I asked, wondering if I was claustrophobic.

'No,' he said, leaning into the space, unscrewing two bolts and pulling two square metal panels from the bottom of it. 'In *here*.'

I peered into an even smaller space.

'The guards at the checkpoint may lift the seat,' he went on, 'looking for smuggled goods . . . But if you are very still, and as quiet as a mouse, they will not know that you are hiding in this place.'

I swallowed hard.

'I will let you out the moment it is safe,' Saul said to comfort me. 'Ten Ks maximum.'

I didn't feel comforted at all.

Saul helped me out of my coat. I climbed into the back of the car and, with a lot of difficulty, twisted myself into the space under the back seat.

'Slide your legs right under, towards the front of the car,' Saul said, pointing to a narrow slot that went forward under the driver's seat.

'In there?' I asked, incredulous. He nodded. I was sweating, despite the freezing night air. For a start, the space looked too small for me to fit into, and I couldn't shake the thought that even if I did fit, I might never get out. Saul might as well have been asking me to climb into my coffin.

'Come on. Quickly now!' Saul ordered. 'André Bruin has travelled in there. Remember that it is preferable to going back to prison.'

It was actually surprisingly easy to slide my legs into the long, narrow space. The floor was smooth, with a padded curve in the floor that fitted my posterior perfectly.

'Put these on,' Saul said, handing me a small headset and a mask. 'It will help your breathing, and we can communicate.'

He reached down into the seat space and turned a small metal wheel. A hiss of air came into the mask.

'Breathe slowly,' Saul said, easing a moulded cushion under my neck. 'Just like scuba diving.'

'Am I crossing the border like this?' I asked through the mask. I thought I might just be able to bear the experience, as long as it meant being free of Domeria at last.

But Saul shook his head. 'No,' he said. 'They are too thorough at the border posts to take that chance. They always look for smugglers, but look even harder for political refugees. But we hope that the guards at the internal checkpoint are feeling sleepy and lazy by this time of night, and will send us quickly on our way. Are you ready?'

I nodded, and Saul gave me a smile, then fitted the two metal panels back in place, a mere centimetre above the tip of the oxygen mask. I forced myself to breathe deeply and slowly in the absolute blackness as I heard the seat being slid into position. The back door slammed, and I felt the car rock as Saul climbed into the driver's seat.

There was a click in the earpiece.

'Are you okay, Isabella?' Saul's voice asked.

'I'm okay,' I quavered.

The engine started and the car began to roll. I hoped Saul would drive more slowly than before.

Coloured shapes swam before my eyes, and

because of the complete absence of light, I was far more sensitive to sounds. The tyres drummed loudly on the road, and I heard pebbles bouncing up and hitting the car beneath me. I could even hear Saul breathing into his microphone.

'Five K to the checkpoint,' he said. 'Is everything all right?'

'I'm fine,' I lied, but in fact I was teetering on the edge of screaming '*Get me out of here*!' I breathed even more deeply to hold the panic down.

'Some rough road is coming,' Saul said.

'Rough road,' I squeaked.

The car body rolled as Saul wove his way along the rough section of road. The tip of my mask struck the metal plate as the car lurched over a pothole.

The ride gradually became smooth again, then Saul whispered, 'I can see the checkpoint lights in the distance. Are you breathing okay?'

'I'm breathing okay,' I said, battling with myself to take slow breaths.

'You must remain silent now, Isabella,' Saul said. 'We are close. No more speaking at all. Only quiet breathing. You hear me?'

'I hear you,' I whispered.

'I am putting the mike away until we are through. Be quiet like a mouse now. Don't move. Do not sneeze. Good luck. Don't worry.'

The headset clicked, and the comforting sound of

Saul's breathing was gone. A whimper started to form in my throat but I bit hard on my lip to stop it.

We pulled to a stop and I could hear muffled shouts. The car rocked as Saul climbed out. The muffled voices came closer. I kept perfectly still, but my heartbeat was thumping in my ears.

More voices. The car moved as the doors were opened. The voices were nearer still.

The car shifted as someone climbed in, and I heard the scrape of boots just above my head. Someone said something in Domerian. Saul replied, laughing. He sounded relaxed.

The boot was opened, and a moment later there was a thump as it slammed shut.

The boots above my head scraped again, and a voice, almost next to my ear, muttered something in Domerian as the back seat was lifted. The muttering was suddenly louder. I stopped breathing. My heart was hammering. The boot crunched down onto the metal panel a centimetre above my nose. I opened my eyes. If this was it, I wanted to see the face of the man who discovered me.

The voice again. Saul laughing in reply.

'Okay,' the voice said, and I felt the seat drop back into place. The boots scraped out of the car.

Saul shouted something in Domerian, and laughed some more.

I started breathing again.

We were standing in the dark, at the edge of another pine forest. The car was two hundred metres behind us, hidden from the road beneath a spread of pine branches. A biting wind was rushing through the trees, and I pulled the collar of my coat high around my ears.

'Wait here,' Saul said, 'I'll go ahead and check. If I am not back in thirty minutes, go back to the road. Stay away from the car. At the road, turn back the way we came. There is a house with a stone gateway that we passed five kilometres back. Wait there until someone comes to fetch you. They are friends, and will look after you.'

I stood against a tree trunk trying to shelter from the wind as Saul disappeared into the night. Holding my hands over my freezing ears, I hoped and hoped that I wouldn't have to walk five kilometres back along a dark road to another lot of people I didn't know. I would never have thought it possible, but right then there was nothing I wanted more than to be a little child again, safe in Dad's arms.

I don't know how long I waited, but eventually Saul returned. 'They are waiting across the border,' he whispered. 'Follow me.'

The wind drove at us like icy spikes. As we stumbled through the darkness I fell over twice, but scrambled back to my feet, petrified of losing Saul. Eventually, a slide down a steep path between two walls of solid rock took us out of the wind and into a narrow gully.

Ahead of us I could see the dim outline of a high chain-link fence.

'This way,' Saul whispered, and headed down the gully along the fence. I scrambled after him. 'Here,' he said.

I looked up, wondering how I was going to climb over this great wall of wire.

'Down here,' Saul whispered. 'Quickly. Underneath. There's a hole. There is a woman to meet you on the other side.'

I got down on my hands and knees, groped around, found the hole and slithered forward. My nose scraped through the dirt as I squeezed under the tight wire. As soon as I was through and brushing the dirt from my face, I remembered the man who had brought me there.

'Saul!' I hissed, clinging onto the wire.

'What is it?'

'Thankyou, Saul. Goodbye.'

The moment I turned away from the fence, a torch flashed further up the slope. I clambered towards it. A young woman in black clothes was waiting amongst the pines.

'This way,' she whispered.

The wind moaned in the tree-tops as I followed her closely. After a long steep climb she pushed me under a tree and went ahead by herself. She came back a few minutes later, dragged me out of my hiding place, and led me to where a small car was parked out of sight between the dark trunks. No interior light came on when she opened the doors.

'You have left Domeria,' she said, starting the engine. 'We'll be at the airport in a few hours.'

I woke up as we were pulling up outside a small airport building. A man came running to open my door, I stepped out, and the woman drove off without a word.

The man led me to the check-in desk, where he placed an airline ticket and a red European Union passport on the counter. The woman behind the counter checked the passport and ticket, looked at me, and passed them back. The man indicated the glass doors that led out onto the runway, where a lone twenty-seater jet was standing. As we passed through the doors he gave me the passport.

'Read the passport,' he said. 'I'll leave you here, but I will watch to see that you get away safely. Remember to read the passport.'

I was strapped into my seat and we were taxiing onto the runway before I remembered to do what the man had told me. The name on the passport was Frances Lewis, and the photo of the blonde-haired young woman looked only a little like me.

19

Saturday Morning

I had just confirmed that the Immigration officer who passed my false passport wasn't following me, when I saw Dad and Alice at the Arrivals gate. Dad threw out his arms and shouted my name. I was in his arms in seconds, and he crushed me so hard I couldn't speak. Then he held me at arm's length and ran his fingers through my blonde hair, muttering 'Isabella! Let me look at you!'

I tried to say, 'Call me Frances,' but I was crying so hard that no words would come out. I buried myself back in Dad's arms where I slowly, very slowly, pulled myself together.

'I've got a lot to tell you,' I finally sniffed, and Alice hugged me gently.

'They phoned to say you've got a plan to get Leo's parents out of gaol,' Dad said, as I rubbed at my eyes with his handkerchief. 'But they don't know what it is,' he added.

'Is there somewhere we can talk?' I asked.

I held onto Dad and Alice as tightly as I could as

we walked through the crowded terminal to a café. We found an empty booth at the back, but it wasn't until Alice had come back with coffee and toast that I could trust myself to speak.

They listened quietly and carefully, and the coffee and toast were long gone by the time I said, 'And that's my plan.'

Dad stared at me. I could see that he didn't think my plan was completely stupid, but I couldn't work out what else he was thinking. 'It would take a shocking lot of organising,' he said at last.

'I could organise it,' Alice said. 'But what do you mean by "open space"?'

'A big open park, free of trees,' I said. 'Maybe a park that one of our family knows well. It'd make the planning easier.'

'Mum knows Greenwich Park like the back of her hand,' said Alice.

'Could Gary organise the recording gear?' Dad asked.

'Without a problem,' Alice said. 'I can't think what we'd do about a luxury car, though. Apart from hiring a Rolls Royce or something.'

'Actually,' Dad said, 'Derek has a friend who collects classic cars.'

Alice started a list. 'Park; recording gear; phone Derek,' she said as she wrote. 'Will we be based at Mum's place?'

I thought back to Nana's flat. 'Definitely not,' I said. 'Nana's place is too small. It's on the second floor, and worst of all, it's only got one way in and out. We could be trapped like—'

'Rats in a barrel,' Dad offered.

'We need accommodation, then,' Alice said, and added it to her list. 'The Clarence Hotel, across the Heath from the park, maybe.'

'That'd do,' said Dad. 'It's—

'Hang on a moment,' I said. 'Dad hasn't agreed to do it yet. Without Dad, there is no plan.'

Dad rubbed his cheek.

'What were the alternative plans?' he asked.

'There weren't any.'

'There's an awful lot of ways it could go badly wrong,' he mused, rubbing his chin. But he was smiling the tiniest of smiles.

'A million ways,' I said. 'More holes than a colander.'

'It'd be a challenge,' Dad nodded.

'But is it a challenge you're prepared to take, Martin?' Alice asked.

'No alternatives, eh?' he checked. I shook my head. 'Well . . . I'd better do it, then.'

I wrapped my arms around his neck and squeezed him. 'I knew you would.'

'Did you?' Dad seemed genuinely surprised.

'Wait a minute, though,' I said. '*You've* agreed.

But there's a whole bunch of people in Domeria who haven't even seen the plan yet. Let alone agreed to it. The plan is pointless without them.'

'You'd better go and phone Leo, then,' Dad said.

Alice was busy talking on her mobile when I came back from calling Leo on a public phone. Dad was nowhere to be seen.

'I've booked some rooms at the Clarence Hotel,' Alice said when she hung up. 'I've spoken to Derek about a posh car from his friend, and Gary is organising radio-mikes, video equipment, and walkie-talkies. I've also phoned your mum to say you're safe again. I woke her up.'

I couldn't believe how quickly my plan was being put into action. 'I told Leo we'd be needing an answer within an hour,' I said.

An hour was an impossibly short time, but if we didn't move fast, the plan might fall apart fast. The smallest leak could destroy the whole thing.

'How many people will come from Domeria?' Alice asked.

I counted quickly. 'There were five of them at the meeting, but Patrice won't come. Four.'

'Nine twin rooms will cover it, then,' said Alice ticking her list. 'I'll call Mum and Jane and invite them all to stay at the Clarence. Even if nothing comes of all this, I suppose we can still do some sightseeing together.'

Dad re-appeared, winding his way between the crowded café tables. I looked twice. An hour and a half ago he had greeted me in a jumper, anorak and jeans. Now he was dressed in a high-buttoned black suit with narrow trousers, a white shirt and a yellow tie.

'What d'you think?' he asked.

'Sharp and expensive,' I said.

'Very expensive,' Dad said. 'I thought I'd better look sharp.'

We still hadn't heard from Leo when our taxi pulled up outside the Clarence Hotel in Blackheath two hours later. I could just imagine Patrice at the meeting table, still shaking his head.

The Clarence Hotel was an elegant three-storey brick building that looked out over the Heath. The almost treeless Heath, where they'd buried bodies during the Black Death nearly four hundred years ago, lay between the Clarence Hotel and Greenwich Park, the location we had chosen for carrying out my plan.

We were carrying our luggage through the front doors when my mobile rang. I dropped my bag and snatched the mobile out of my pocket.

'Isabella,' Leo said, his voice echoing down the line. 'We have come to a decision at last. We have been talking without cease since I opened your envelope, and Patrice had many objections. But we will do it.'

'It's on,' I said to Dad and Alice, who were standing there with their eyes fixed on me.

'But has Johann Feld agreed to come to London?' I asked. The plan was pointless without his participation.

'Otto organised for him to be rung fifteen minutes ago. Feld was very greedy to take up the offer, and said he and a colleague will come to negotiate. He was told that we would inform him of the meeting place in due course.'

The first few parts of my plan had actually clicked into place. 'When can you guys get here?' I asked.

'If we don't have problems leaving Domeria, we can be at London City Airport within five hours. Where will we go to from there?' he asked.

'Alice will give you directions. See you tonight.' I passed my mobile to Alice.

I was thrilled and filled with dread at the same time. I almost wished that Patrice had won the argument, and that my plan had died before it even began, because now I was suddenly responsible for putting people I loved in possible danger of their lives.

Nana, Aunty Jane and Sam arrived after lunch, quietly grim about the serious work that might be ahead of us. While Jane helped Alice to organise things at the hotel, Sam, Dad, Nana and I went for a walk around the upper section of Greenwich Park to make sure that it fitted the requirements of my plan. No sooner had we walked through the gates than I saw the perfect location: a wide, open area of grass surrounded by trees.

I ticked item one on my mental list.

Blackheath Avenue ran from the park gates all the way to the Royal Observatory and the statue of General Wolfe at the centre of the park. It was wide and straight, and skirted one side of the grassed area. It would allow us a fast get-away if things went pear-shaped.

I ticked item two.

My plan also required us to be able to lose ourselves in a crowd. Even though it was a winter afternoon, tourist groups and single sightseers were strolling along Blackheath Avenue and milling about the Royal Observatory, the statue of General Wolfe, and the cafés that were dotted about the park. Plenty of cars were parked along Blackheath Avenue and in the other parking areas. These cars would provide cover for our van.

Item three was covered.

Item four was that the park had to be large enough to provide separate areas for the three stages of my plan. When Nana informed us that Greenwich Park was 163 acres and had, among other things, a Rose Garden, a Deer Reserve, bandstands, as well as the cafés and museums, I mentally ticked item four as well.

It was almost dark by the time we had finished surveying the park. We caught a taxi back across the Heath to the Clarence Hotel.

Alice was on the front steps watching for Gary. 'He'll be here any minute,' she said. 'And Derek's just phoned. His friend will let us borrow his best car.'

Another piece of my plan was in place.

A moment later Gary pulled into the carpark.

'Welcome home from prison, Isabella!' he said, jumping out of the van. 'Come and look at the gear.' He slid the back door open. 'Mixing desk.' He pointed to the sloping panel of sliders, knobs and meters that sat on a new shelf behind the front seats. 'Radio-mike receivers. Six radio-mikes, batteries, et cetera are in the black case there. Most important, one quality digital video camera.' Gary tapped another plastic case. 'Ten times optical, and one-twenty times digital zoom. We could video a rat across the far side of the park with this wizard piece of technology,' he said, rubbing the case affectionately. 'And last, but definitely not least, eight walkie-talkies with a range of four miles.'

20

Dad and I were sprawled in the antique armchairs of
the shadowy first floor guest lounge. It was seven
thirty, and we were worried. Leo had said they'd be
at London City Airport five hours after he phoned.
They were now two hours late, and there had been
no word from him.

I had spent the last hour trying to recalculate
the plan in my head, to see if we could manage
without the Domerians if they didn't arrive. I'd run
through, over and over, what I thought the
difficulties might be, and now my brain was starting
to overheat.

The only definite part of the plan we had at this
point, apart from rooms at the hotel and the
equipment that Alice and Gary had organised, was
that Johann Feld would be arriving at some time the
following afternoon, expecting to do a deal. And if
Leo and the others failed to arrive, we'd be fronting
up to Feld without Otto and Peter, the two security
agents we were counting on to turn my plan from

amateur experiment to a professional operation.

Why was Leo late? My plan had been known for seven or eight hours maximum. Could the Domerian government have found out about it already? Maybe Leo and the others had been held up by a snowstorm in Domeria. Or bad weather had delayed the plane. Or maybe the checkpoint guards had discovered one of them in the secret compartment of the Mercedes? Perhaps we would have to undertake the plan without them.

Then my mobile rang.

I almost shouted with relief when I heard Leo's voice. 'Where are you?'

'London City Airport. We've had a very difficult time. Peter was arrested in Domeria.'

'Arrested?'

'They seemed to know what our movements would be. Peter and Helena were travelling together when they apprehended Peter, but Helena managed to get away. Patrice, Otto and I went another way, but we had to abandon the car and walk a long way to the border.'

'Did you say Patrice?' I asked.

'Yes. He didn't like your plan, but he insisted on coming.'

'But are you safe now?'

'We think so. Helena and Otto are on their way to you as we speak. Patrice and I watched to see if they were followed. We will leave soon. I must go now. Goodbye.'

Dad was sitting up straight in his chair, listening hard to my side of the conversation.

'They're in trouble, Dad,' I said.

'We're in trouble too, then.'

'Leo says the Domerian Government knew their moves.'

'Or he's nervous, and just thinks they do.'

'Peter has been arrested,' I said.

'It could be a coincidence.'

'Leo, Otto and Patrice had some trouble too. They had to abandon their car.'

'It might still be a coincidence,' Dad said, but he didn't sound as confident.

'Or they're bringing a spy with them.'

'Is that how you see it?'

'Only the people who were at the meeting were to see my plan,' I explained. 'And all the people at the meeting, except for Peter, are coming here.'

'So do we abandon the plan?' Dad asked.

'I don't know what to do, except carry on with it for now.'

The lounge door opened and Sam came in. 'We're ready,' she said.

'For what?' I asked.

'Come and look,' Dad said, standing up and grabbing my hand. 'We'll get the full story from

Helena soon enough when she arrives.'

We followed Sam out of the guest lounge and along to Dad's room.

While Dad and I had been waiting in the guest lounge, a few changes had taken place. In front of the long window that looked out over the Heath, and posed as though for a photograph, were Alice, Jane and Derek, smartly dressed in black suits. Their expressions of cold cruel calm gave them a particularly sinister look.

'This is the gang, Isabella,' Nana said from her armchair. 'As per your instructions, they are a murderous gang of immense criminal power and money.'

'Dirty money,' said Gary.

'That needs laundering,' added Sam.

'And there is a country called Domeria,' I said, 'from which a money-hungry man called Johann Feld will come tomorrow to offer such a service.'

'And let it be his downfall!' said Nana grandly.

'But there is a problem,' I said. I explained about Peter's arrest, and the difficulties that Leo and his team had getting out of Domeria.

'So they may be bringing a traitor into our midst,' mused Nana. 'Any suspicions, Isabella?'

A picture of Patrice slotted into my mind, but Patrice was too obvious a candidate. Unless he was playing a double double game with us.

The phone on the bedside table rang. Dad picked it up.

'Two of our guests have arrived,' he said. 'Isabella and I will go and meet them. It's ten past eight now. Let us assume that our second lot of guests will be here soon. We'll re-gather in the guest lounge for our final meeting at nine thirty sharp.'

Helena and Otto were waiting at the hotel desk. Helena looked pale and exhausted, although Otto seemed calm and contained.

I wondered whether one of them was our traitor.

'You're here at last,' I said.

'But Peter is not,' Helena said, pushing her dark hair away from her face.

'Leo and Patrice will join us as soon as they think it's safe to leave the airport,' said Otto.

Dad fetched their keys from the concierge and we escorted them to their rooms. Otto asked to share with Leo. 'For Leo's protection,' he said.

Helena had a room to herself.

'Our final briefing will be at nine thirty in the guest lounge,' Dad repeated, as we left Helena in her room.

She nodded, then closed and locked her door.

Otto, however, wanted to survey the hotel's security. He and I inspected the hotel from top to bottom, checking exits and fire escapes, staircases, empty bedrooms, the kitchen, the laundry and storage rooms. At first I thought he was being unnecessarily fussy, until he began to point out the great number of ways a person could sneak in other than by the front doors.

As we entered each room, Otto stood in the doorway and seemed to take a mental picture of what he saw. Then he pulled back curtains, looked under the beds, checked inside the wardrobes and cupboards, and opened every door and window. As we performed the inspection, I recounted every detail of my plan, and explained the arrangements that had already been put in place.

With a flick of a tiny metal tool, Otto re-locked the door of a storeroom filled with stacks of chairs. 'So, Isabella,' he said, 'do you suspect that your plan has been leaked?'

'Maybe it's just coincidence,' I said.

'Perhaps,' he said.

'If it *was* leaked it has to be someone who had access to my plan. That narrows the field.' I knew that the field of candidates was narrowed to five people, three of whom I thought I knew and trusted, and one of whom was standing right beside me.

'Except that Patrice had photocopies made by one of the staff,' Otto told me.

I gasped. 'But he's the Chief of Security!'

Otto nodded grimly. 'So the field of candidates is larger than we originally thought,' he said.

'Do we give up?' I asked.

'We will be forced to, if Johann Feld does not arrive tomorrow. But until then we should continue as if everything is in place. In the interim our mole, if there is one, might even reveal himself.'

As we headed down the stairs, we heard the front doors open and voices come up from below. Patrice and Leo were at the hotel desk. Like Helena, they both looked grey and exhausted. Otto immediately pulled Patrice aside and began a whispered conversation.

Dad joined us and organised a second key to Leo and Otto's room. Otto and Patrice were still deep in discussion, as we took Leo upstairs.

'Guest lounge at nine thirty, please,' I said as we passed them. 'And you need to make that phone call.'

They nodded.

We were all gathered at one end of the guest lounge.

'As a working title, we'll call ourselves the Greenwich Gang,' I began. 'The Greenwich Gang is a family organisation,' I went on. 'Dad is the boss. Alice, Jane and Derek are the lieutenants. We are rich, we make a lot of money from drugs, prostitution, people smuggling and small-arms sales.

We make a lot of bad money that needs laundering.'

'Which is why we are of interest to Johann Feld and his colleague,' said Dad.

'Who will be coming to Greenwich Park tomorrow afternoon,' I continued, 'as the result of two phone calls made by a contact of Otto's, one from Domeria earlier today, and one from here in England about a half-hour ago. They are coming to arrange the transfer of some of our money to them, in exchange for the rest of our criminal money being laundered in Domeria. Greenwich Park is where we've told them we want to make the deal.'

'The reason we're in the park,' said Gary, 'is that I can get good sound and images there without having to set up a house, flat or some other building. The logistics of setting up an interior space with sound and video surveillance equipment for tomorrow were not possible.'

Otto nodded. 'It will also be easier to get away if things go wrong,' he said. 'Tomorrow morning Isabella, her grandmother and I will tour the park, so that I may check the geographical decisions that have been made, and also see the layout of the park for myself.'

'I've managed to get a topographical map and an aerial photograph to assist us,' Alice said.

'Gary should tell us about the sound and video equipment,' said Dad.

Gary cleared his throat. 'The main reason that the recording gear is installed in our van is because it is both concealed and mobile. Also, our van can easily pass for a back-packer vehicle among all the other tourist cars in the park.'

Otto was nodding his approval as Gary continued. 'I'm going to record the sound and images digitally, of course. I've got everything we need: radio-mikes, video-equipment, recording gear, back-up gear, etc. But I would like someone who has had good experience with video cameras. I could do it, but I'd prefer to keep my hands free.'

'I've done a little video stuff at school,' said Sam.

'A little video stuff from you may have to do, then,' said Gary.

'I have had considerable experience with video-camera technology,' said Patrice from the back of the room. Leo turned in his chair to scrutinise Patrice.

It suddenly occurred to me that the position behind the video camera was the perfect place from which to sabotage the plan. I turned to Gary. 'You'll keep a total eye on things, won't you?' I said.

'You bet,' he said. 'You're my man, then, Patrice,' he added.

I couldn't tell whether Patrice was happy to be Gary's man or not. I knew I wasn't comfortable with the idea of Patrice playing such a fundamental role.

'To finish up,' Gary said, 'I've borrowed eight

walkie-talkies, and I can feed any sound we receive through those as well. I'll organise a separate channel on the walkie-talkies, that will transmit from the radio-mikes, so that we can swap channels to either talk to each other, or to listen to the actors at any time.'

'May I see the equipment after the meeting?' Otto asked. 'I have done this work before.'

Gary nodded.

'Transport,' I said. 'Derek, do you want to tell us what's happening on that front?'

'Just so we have the right sort of look for a bunch of rich criminals,' he said, 'I've borrowed a classic American car from a pal of mine. The only condition, apart from not putting a scratch on it, is that I am the only one to drive it. It's a nice vehicle. I think it'll really do the trick.'

I picked up the metre-square aerial map that Alice had organised, and rested it on the mantelpiece.

'And last of all, the most important part: the role that each of us will be playing tomorrow . . .'

21

Otto, Dad, Nana and I borrowed Derek's car and drove through a cold and foggy Greenwich Park just after dawn. The planning meeting had wound up just after eleven, and I was feeling pretty good after six and a half hours of solid sleep.

Otto made me repeat the details of my plan all over again, as we followed its route from Location One, the Rose Garden in the south-east of the park; via Location Two, the statue of General Wolfe outside the old buildings of the Royal Observatory; to Location Three, the open grassed area off Blackheath Avenue where the main action was going to happen.

Nana was our encyclopaedia. As well as knowing the long history of the park, she also knew the geography of its slopes and buildings like the back of her hand.

Otto insisted that we stay in the car.

'Johann Feld and his colleague will bring field agents with them. The agents may well be making their own reconnaissance even now,' he said.

My stress level, which was already high, rose another notch. Not that we saw anyone, except for a tall man walking two poodles.

'Could he be a field agent?' I asked, pointing to the poodle walker.

'They would not have had time to organise dogs as cover,' Otto said.

'And they'll probably stay out of sight?' Dad asked.

'Probably,' Otto nodded.

Nana was silent. I guessed she was seeing her beloved Greenwich Park in a new light: the setting for espionage work, rather than Sunday strolls.

A pale wet sun was appearing through the clouds as we drove back across the Heath to the hotel. Helena, Sam and Patrice were eating breakfast in the empty dining room, the others were still upstairs, and Leo had left for the airport thirty minutes earlier, because it was his task to phone us as soon as Johann Feld landed. Derek had already gone, too, in a taxi to pick up the car. He'd arranged to park it out of sight at a petrol station around the corner until we needed it.

My stomach wasn't feeling in any shape to receive food, but I had some toast and orange juice anyway before going upstairs with Sam.

There was nothing left to do but wait. All the planning was in place.

'Are you sorry you spoke to Leo on the plane?' Sam asked as we reached my room.

She had tapped straight into my thoughts. The idea of a simple, even boring, holiday amongst my relatives seemed magically attractive.

'Of course not,' I lied, then added, 'Maybe a little.'

'They give people medals for doing a lot less,' she said.

'Do you want to play cards?' I asked. I needed to do *something*.

Sam had just dealt the first hand of Gin Rummy when there was a crash of footsteps in the hall. We threw our cards onto the bed and jumped up as the door flew open. It was Dad.

'They've landed!' he said. 'Johann Feld, and someone called Igor Mann. Otto swore and Patrice went white when they heard who it was.'

'Because?' I asked. My heart was thumping twice as hard as it had been five seconds before.

'Igor Mann is the boss of the Domerian Government Security Services. The most important spy in Domeria.'

Back down in the dining room, I discovered that Derek and the car were already on their way, due to arrive in about five minutes. The recording van was ready, too, and Dad, Alice and Jane had their radio-mikes on and working.

Sam and I stood with our backs to Gary while

he clipped the microphone transmitter boxes onto our waistbands, and positioned the tiny microphones, hidden in our clothes.

Dad had gone very quiet, all his attention turned inward. He was becoming the man he was going to have to be in Greenwich Park.

I glanced at Patrice and Helena. It was hard to believe that either of them could be the one who had betrayed us. But why had Patrice, a professional security person who should have known better, allowed copies of my secret plan to be made? Surely that made him the prime suspect? At least I knew it wasn't Helena. She had travelled halfway around the world and back with Leo, and had been abducted and imprisoned in the course of trying to keep him safe.

But did that mean that Peter was the mole? Was his arrest yesterday in Domeria just a ruse to mislead us? Mislead us in what way, though? We were in England, he was in Domeria. Was his role as a guard in Mont Noir really his true self?

'Isy!' Gary's voice broke into my thoughts.

'What?'

'You were daydreaming,' he said gently. 'Now remember, this radio-mike is only one-way. I'll be able to hear you, but you'll need to use a walkie-talkie or a mobile to conduct a two-way conversation. Feel the transmitter box for the on/off switch.'

He placed my finger on the black box in the middle of my back.

'I've got it,' I said, clicking the switch up and down.

'I'll go out to the van and check your signals. Come with me, Patrice,' Gary called over his shoulder. 'You too, Helena.'

'Otto,' I said. 'Tell me about Igor Mann.'

'Of all the people in Domeria,' Otto said calmly, 'Igor Mann is perhaps the cleverest that could be operating against us.'

'We'll have to be even cleverer, then,' said Dad.

'Igor will have sent in field agents last night. I know how he operates. I used to work for him.'

I stared unbelievingly at Otto.

'It will be very much to our advantage that you know how he thinks,' stated Nana.

Otto bowed his head in agreement.

'Of course!' I said. 'I just needed a moment to think it through. Nana, you've got your mobile, too?'

She pulled her pink mobile from her handbag and waved it at me. 'Good luck, my darlings,' she said, as she rose and headed out of the door. I was sure I heard a break in her voice.

Alice and I were watching from the dining-room window as Gary drove the van out. Two minutes later, with Derek at the wheel, a long, sleek, winged yellow car with dazzlingly bright chrome bumper bars cruised into the carpark. Dad came and stood behind me, staring down at the glittering yellow vision.

'I'd better be going,' he said.

I grabbed him, and hugged him hard. 'Be careful, Dad,' I said.

'I will. And you remember to run for your life if things go wrong.' He kissed me once on each cheek.

'That applies to us all,' said Alice.

'Take care, Martin,' Jane said, from the table. 'I'll hug you afterwards.' Otto just nodded.

I watched Dad go down the front steps and climb into the yellow car. As it pulled out of the carpark I said a silent prayer. Derek and Dad were going to park in a prearranged spot nearby until they were needed.

'Leo says they have just left the airport,' Otto said from across the room. 'Depending on how long they have to wait for the ferry, they may be at the park inside thirty minutes.' He stood up, pocketed his mobile, then picked up four walkie-talkies and a small pair of binoculars from the table. 'It's time for us to go, too,' he said. 'They were trying to catch us out by arriving early. But we are ready for them.'

Alice, Jane, Sam, Otto and I climbed into Derek's white Ford. Otto was at the wheel. It was still early, so the usually busy roads were almost empty, and we were across the Heath and through the park gates within five minutes.

A light wind had come up, and there was no sign of the morning's fog as we cruised down Blackheath Avenue past the signs to the Royal Observatory and Maritime Museum, then on towards the statue of General Wolfe.

Otto picked up the walkie-talkie from the seat beside him. 'Otto here. Are you receiving, Gary?'

'Receiving you fine. We're stationed outside the park gates watching for our guests to arrive. Over.'

'We're heading for Location One, the Rose Garden. Perhaps we'll see some of Igor Mann's agents, if we are lucky and they are careless. Over and out.'

We turned right off Blackheath Avenue onto a smaller road, passed a bandstand, and then pulled up behind two parked cars between two stands of bare-branched oak trees. We were within two hundred metres of the Rose Garden.

'Alice, Isabella and I will watch from here,' Otto said. 'Jane and Samantha, I want you to get out and walk closer to the Rose Garden. Take this walkie-talkie,' he said, handing one to Jane. 'Use the earpiece and microphone, it's more discreet.'

Jane and Sam climbed out. Jane fitted the earpiece and mike from the walkie-talkie and tested it. Her voice came loud and clear from one of the other walkie-talkies on the seat beside Otto.

'Skirt the perimeter of the Rose Garden,' Otto said into his walkie-talkie, as Sam and Jane began to walk away. 'But stay in sight, and stay clear of the bushes. Over.'

'Got that. Over,' said Jane, as they headed toward the Rose Garden.

Otto, Alice and I sat back in the warmth of the car and watched Jane and Sam stroll towards the curved-wire fence that separated the Rose Garden from the rest of the park.

'There are two women with a dog. Over,' Jane said at one point.

'Copy that,' Otto said.

'A man with a child on a tricycle. Over,' Jane said a few minutes later.

'There's someone coming along the Deer Reserve fence towards us,' Jane whispered. 'Over.'

No sooner had Jane spoken, than Gary's voice crackled into the car.

'Here they come! Patrice tells me that Johann and his Igor have just driven into the Park. There's a driver with them, too. Over.'

'Copy that, Gary,' Otto said. 'Jane and Sam come straight back. We're starting to happen. Over.'

My heart seemed to leap into my throat, but Otto remained stern and calm. I tried to follow his example and managed to swallow my heart again.

Alice breathed out a long slow breath beside me.

'We'll assume the driver is one of them. Over.'

'We can see they've taken the right turn towards the bandstand. Over.' Gary said. This meant that Johann and Igor's car was now approaching us.

Jane and Sam climbed back in. 'I think we were being watched by a man,' said Sam with a shiver.

'I think he saw us, just before we left the fence,' said Jane. 'We were out of sight as we came back through the oaks, though.'

'Either way, it doesn't matter,' said Otto, continuing to look out through the windscreen. 'Now they know that we also have people on the ground. Here come Johann and Igor.' Otto pointed through the windscreen to a black BMW that was pulling up near the bandstand three hundred metres beyond the oaks.

I grabbed the binoculars from the front seat and trained them on the car.

There was a twenty-second pause, and then a front door opened slowly and the driver climbed out. Standing between the door and the body of the car, he scanned the area around him. Then I watched him put his head back into the car, and the two rear doors opened.

'Igor Mann this side, Johann Feld the other,' Otto said quietly, as two men in overcoats stepped out. Igor Mann was tall and thin, with glasses and cropped hair. As the driver had done, Igor Mann stayed between the car door and the body of the car while he surveyed the territory.

I shifted the binoculars to look at Johann Feld. He was shorter, with more hair than Igor, and seemed to be cowering behind the body of the car.

Igor turned and talked to the driver. The driver nodded. Then Igor came out from behind his door and slammed it shut. He walked around behind the car, pulled Johann away from his door, and slammed it too. The two men began to walk towards the Rose Garden.

Otto nodded. 'As we discussed last night, we'll give them two minutes to establish themselves, then Jane and Alice, you can go and tell them that the location for the meeting has changed.'

'Switch on your radio-mikes,' I said.

'Keep your walkie-talkie,' said Otto.

'Tell them the location for the meeting has changed for reasons of security,' Otto said, turning to Jane and Alice. 'Don't answer any questions. Just tell them to follow you when you signal. And leave plenty of space between you and them before you signal. We don't know how many agents Igor has on the ground, so keep out in the open as much as possible. As you know, you must lead them to Location Two at the statue of General Wolfe.'

Alice and Jane reached behind their backs and

switched on the mike packs beneath their jackets. They glanced at Otto, who nodded, and they climbed out of the car. A gust of wind hit them just as they entered the stand of oaks.

A walkie-talkie hissed. 'Gary here. We're parking in the middle of a line of seven cars on Blackheath Avenue, opposite Location Three. What's happening your side? Over.'

Otto picked up the walkie-talkie. 'Gary, you should have a signal now from Alice and Jane. Please confirm. Over.'

Gary's voice. 'Confirm that. Good signal. I can hear them talking to each other. Over.'

Otto continued with his instructions. 'Helena, leave the van now and walk towards the Rose Garden. Watch for anyone shadowing Johann and Igor as they follow Alice and Jane to the statue. Over.'

'We've got that,' said Gary. 'Helena is heading off. Over.'

'Derek, this is Otto. Standby with Martin and the yellow car. Your position will be halfway between the gates and the Wolfe statue. You'll see the recording van, but don't draw attention to it. Over.'

'Confirm that. Standing by. Over,' Derek replied.

I still had the binoculars. 'Igor and Johann are looking around for us, Otto,' I said. Then I saw Johann gesture impatiently at Igor. Igor gestured for Johann to calm down, and then pointed over his shoulder. Johann turned to see Alice and Jane approaching.

'Time for you and Sam to go to General Wolfe,' said Otto, glancing at me in the rear vision mirror. 'Switch on your radio-mike, and take a walkie-talkie.'

The walkie-talkie hissed as he handed it to me. 'Channel Four is for receiving radio-mike signals,' said Gary. 'Channel One remains for general two-way communication.' I watched Otto click a switch on top of one of his walkie-talkies and looked at mine and did the same to Channel Four. I had just pushed the earpiece into my ear when Jane spoke.

'Mr Feld?' she asked sharply. I imagined it was the voice she used with difficult passengers.

'Who are you?' a man's voice asked.

'That's Igor,' said Otto quietly.

'We're here to guide you to the location of the meeting, gentlemen,' Alice said firmly, as if she thought them rude to have asked. 'Please remain here until I signal you to follow.'

'It was arranged that we would meet here,' said another man's voice.

'Johann,' said Otto.

'For reasons of security we have changed arrangements.' This was Jane.

I watched Johann and Igor look from Jane to Alice. 'If the coast is clear,' Alice said, 'we will signal for you to follow us. If you continue to follow us at the same distance, we will warn you of any problems, should they occur.'

'I would have thought you would have made sure that no problems could occur,' Johann said.

'We always expect the unexpected,' said Jane, and she and Alice turned and walked away.

Jane's voice came over Channel Four on the walkie-talkie. 'If you can't see us, Otto, we're walking away now. They're staying put like good boys. When we're opposite the bandstand, we'll signal them to follow. Do you have any new instructions for us?'

As Alice and Jane went out of sight, followed by Igor and Johann, the black BMW that had brought the two men did a U-turn and drove away. Otto nodded, and Sam and I slid out of the car and headed west to General Wolfe.

As we walked I clicked back to Channel One. Otto's voice filled my left ear.

'Otto to Alice and Jane. Over.'

There was a pause.

'Jane here. Over.'

'As soon as you arrive at General Wolfe,' Otto said, 'take the steps down from the Observatory clock and disappear. Keep out of sight until called for. Over.'

'Okay, I've got that,' said Jane. 'Over.'

Then another voice came over the radio.

'Helena here. I'm reporting one extra man coming out of cover near the Deer Reserve. Now there's a second. They're following Igor and Johann.'

'Copy that, Helena. Over,' said Otto.

Sam and I were heading cross-country towards the statue. On the slope above us, two hundred metres away, we caught occasional glimpses of Alice and Jane leading Igor and Johann over the longer route along the main paths.

We reached the statue of General Wolfe within a couple of minutes. Even though a cold wind was gusting up the hill, a group of six tourists was leaning over the safety rail, taking videos of the London skyline and the River Thames in the distance.

Sam went and tucked herself in beside the tourists. I crossed into the courtyard of the Royal Observatory and hid to one side of the brick wall beside the gates. Despite my newly blonde hair and eyebrows, I was still taking care to hide from any field agents who might recognise me from Piccadilly Circus or my abduction.

All that Sam had to say when Johann and Igor arrived was, 'Walk along Blackheath Avenue, and you will be met'. As soon as she'd said it, she was to descend the same steps from the Observatory clock that Alice and Jane had taken.

I caught sight of Alice and Jane.

'Alice and Jane are twenty metres from the statue now,' I said into my mike. 'Johann and Igor are twenty metres behind them.'

Alice and Jane reached the statue, and Jane signalled for the men to wait at the base of it.

Johann said something to Igor, and Igor shrugged.

Alice and Jane passed within a metre of me on the far side of the wall, then descended the steps to the lower section of the Park.

When Igor and Johann reached the statue a moment later, Sam stepped out from the group of tourists and spoke her line. Johann looked at her in surprise, so she repeated it, and pointed along Blackheath Avenue towards the park gates.

Suddenly, Johann grabbed Sam by the wrist. She twisted and pulled, but couldn't get her wrist free. I was about to run out and help, when Igor placed his hand on Johann's hand and plucked it off Sam's wrist. Johann turned angrily to Igor, and Sam made a run for it, past me and down the steps after Alice and Jane.

'Sam's away and safe,' I muttered into the walkie-talkie. 'Johann and Igor are heading towards Location Three. Johann seems angry, but Igor's staying cool. Over.'

'Copy that, Isabella. Over,' said Otto.

I stayed where I was, peering out from behind

the wall, and saw two burly men in overcoats turn up, glance briefly at the group of tourists, then follow Johann and Igor.

'I think two agents are also approaching Location Three. They're going for the cover of the trees on the east side of Blackheath Avenue,' I reported. 'I'm following. Over.'

'Copy that, Isabella,' said Otto. 'Time to move, Derek. Yellow car to the Park now, please. Over.'

I waited half a minute, then left the safety of my brick wall and slipped out through the gates. I hung back until the field agents reached the trees on the far side of Blackheath Avenue. Then, under the cover of the same trees, I followed them.

22

Johann and Igor arrived at Location Three just as the gleaming American car cruised through the park gates. The sight of it made them stop dead in their tracks. The field agents, two hundred metres ahead of me, were equally mesmerised. Glowing yellow in the grey morning light, the car seemed to illuminate Blackheath Avenue.

The hood was folded down. Derek, in his dark suit and sunglasses, was at the steering wheel, while Dad, in his black suit, white shirt and yellow tie, was alone in the back seat. The car pulled slowly to a stop, seeming to hover for a moment before finally coming to rest.

Igor recovered from his surprise and walked towards the car. Derek switched the engine off and climbed out, then tilted his seat forward. Dad stepped out onto the road and Igor and Dad eyed each other across the long yellow bonnet.

I reached down and clicked my walkie-talkie back to Channel Four.

'You Johann Feld?' Dad asked, in a voice I'd never heard him use before. It was sharp enough to cut your ears, and I was shocked to find myself momentarily afraid of him.

Igor beckoned Johann forward. 'This is Johann Feld,' he said.

'And you are?' Dad's voice cut again.

'Igor Mann. You are?'

'You can call me John.'

Igor nodded, and pointed to the car. 'It's a Desoto Firedome?'

'1957 Desoto Fireflite,' said Dad. '341 cubic inch V8 Hemi.'

I was amazed. Dad knows nothing about cars.

'Very beautiful. I have a '59 Silver Hawk myself.'

'Nice vehicle,' said Dad, and I almost believed he knew what he was talking about. 'I see we are people with shared interests. Perhaps we will be able to do business.'

'Perhaps,' said Igor.

The two of them were sparring, circling and checking each other out.

'Well, let us get on with it, then,' said Johann. 'You can have all the American cars you want, Igor, if we talk successfully.'

'We'll walk and talk,' said Dad, indicating the grass on the other side of the road. 'Let's give ourselves some breathing space.'

This was it! Whatever happened in the next fifteen minutes, good or bad, would probably determine the future of Leo's parents. Maybe of Domeria.

Then I remembered that Patrice was in charge of the videotaping.

I clicked to Channel One and pressed the button on my walkie-talkie.

'Gary, can you talk?' I asked. 'Over.'

'Make it quick, Isabella. Over.'

'Are you watching the videotaping? Over.'

'Patrice is an expert, Isy. Beautiful sound and images. Gotta go. Over and out.'

I crossed my fingers. There was nothing more I could do.

I tucked myself behind a hedge and clicked back to Channel Four. I was trembling. I could scarcely believe that I had arranged for my father to be alone in the middle of a park with these two dangerous men. I scanned the trees around me, searching for the field agents that I was also responsible for having brought to this park. I couldn't see them. I scanned again. They'd disappeared.

Dad's voice came into my ear.

'I was overjoyed to hear that the Domerian government is modifying its banking laws,' he said.

Johann spoke. 'We are removing blockages. As the European Union becomes stricter about financial transactions, we are steering our country in the opposite direction.'

'It is so much more troublesome to deal with our profits now.' This was Dad. 'A few years ago, a trip to Paris or Hamburg and a new bank account was all one needed to convert profits into usable money. These days, it is far messier and far more expensive. This does not make me happy.'

'And we are the people who can help you,' Johann said eagerly.

'So I understand,' said Dad. 'My Italian and German connections assure me that you are useful people to do business with.'

'Italian and German, you say?' Igor said. 'You will know, then, that we are as good as our word.'

'Put simply,' Dad said, 'if you provide the necessary facilities, then I will make sure that you are very well rewarded.'

'Excellent!' said Johann.

'We understand each other,' said Igor.

There was a pause before Dad's voice slid again like a cold knife into my ear. 'However, I dislike complications,' he said. 'I need our arrangement to be as simple and flexible as possible.'

'Yes, yes,' Johann agreed.

'And I know that the more generous I am, the smoother the path will be. What I propose is . . .' Dad paused again.

The pause was so long that I switched the walkie-talkie off and on and fiddled with the volume control, thinking that it had stopped working. But at last Dad's voice came from the earpiece again.

'What I propose,' he repeated, 'is that I give you thirty percent of the net money that passes satisfactorily through your banking system. Once it is confirmed that my money has become usable, I will transfer that thirty per cent to whichever bank you nominate. A Swiss bank perhaps? Some of the West Indian banks are also most obliging. But the final resting-place of the money is entirely up to you, of course. Some people even prefer their profits in cash, and I am happy to provide suitcases, if that is what you prefer.'

'Thirty percent!' Johann sounded shocked. 'It is generous. I am most sure that we can do business.'

'More than satisfactory,' said Igor.

'If you're happy, I'm well pleased,' said Dad. 'But,' I held my breath waiting for the next part of my plan to unfold. 'André and Theresa Bruin remain a concern to me.'

Suddenly, an unforgettable check-patterned hat caught my eye. I blinked. I shifted my position behind the hedge to get a better view. It was Erik Booré! He was two hundred metres away, between me and the park gates, strolling along the row of parked cars towards the van. With almost imperceptible turns of his head, he was giving the interior of each car he passed a thorough inspection.

'The Bruins!' said Johann in my ear. 'Unhappily, André and Theresa do not comprehend where their best interests lie. It was necessary to remove them from the political equation.'

Erik Booré was twenty-five or thirty vehicles south of the van. At the rate he was going, he would be peering into the van's windows within three or four minutes.

I clicked to Channel One. 'Gary, we've got a problem! Over.'

'Not now, Isabella!' the walkie-talkie hissed.

'Erik Booré is walking along the line of cars towards you! Over.'

'God help us!' The volume of Gary's reply hurt my ear. 'Distract him! You'll have to distract him, Isabella! Over and out.'

'Otto here, Isabella,' the walkie-talkie hissed again. 'I'm on the far side of the park. I'm being watched. I can't get to you quickly. As Gary says, you'll have to distract him. Over and out.'

Distract him? I clicked back to Channel Four, hoping to hear that the deal was sealed and that Gary could drive away. But Dad was calmly stating that Domerians were protesting on the streets.

'There are protests at the Bruins' imprisonment,'

Johann agreed. 'We will need to quieten those protests down, of course. But Igor can fill you in on the details of the action we will take. It is not a large problem.'

How was I to distract Erik?

First, I needed to be closer to him.

Keeping low, I slid out from my hiding place and scurried deeper into the cover of the trees. Then I turned and trotted forward, parallel to Blackheath Avenue and the row of cars that Erik was inspecting. Keeping my eyes peeled for the field agents, and slipping from tree to tree, I came to a position not more than twenty metres away from Erik. I checked around for a tree with low branches and some sort of cover where I could hide. Erik was now less than a hundred metres from the van.

Igor spoke, his voice devoid of emotion. 'The people will forget the Bruins soon enough. The evidence we are manufacturing against them is growing every day. Before this month is out, André and his wife will be entirely discredited.'

I climbed under the low branches of a pine tree, pushing my way through spider-webs until I was hidden. I pushed a hole through the greenery to keep Erik in view. He was spending a long time inspecting an orange sports car.

But I couldn't think how to distract him.

'*Think!*' I hissed to myself. Think, or your plan

will be for nothing. Think of Leo's parents in prison and think of *something*!

Erik had finished inspecting the sports car, and was adjusting the collar of his coat.

I had an idea! Maybe Alice, Jane and Sam...? I needed to keep listening on Channel Four, so I pulled my mobile out and speed-dialled Alice's number.

She answered straight away.

'Where are you?' I asked. 'I need some help.'

'Just coming back up the stairs to General Wolfe. What do you need us to do?'

'Nothing. You're too far away.' I hung up, desperately disappointed.

Erik was peering through the driver's window of a white station wagon.

Dad was in my ear again. 'I have thought long and hard about the Bruins.' The coldness of his voice made me shiver. 'I require a safer solution than imprisonment.'

'What are you proposing?' Igor asked.

Distract Erik!

I couldn't think of anything.

So I called his name.

He didn't react. I thought he hadn't heard, but then he stopped and looked around. After a moment, he shrugged and turned back to the cars.

He was twenty cars from the van now. I watched, paralysed, as he inspected four more.

Then I snapped out of it and yelled, 'Hey you!'

He spun round and looked into the group of trees where I was hiding.

'The Bruins are a complication that I am not prepared to live with.' Dad was stating a simple fact. 'By your own admission, they are not without support. What worries me is that just a little more protest could drive your government from the country. And where would that leave me?'

'We have them secure,' Igor said. 'We are building a case against them.'

'That is all very well,' said Dad.

'What are you suggesting?' Johann asked.

Erik was sixteen cars from the van, standing still with his head tilted towards me.

Dad's voice had become ice. 'Let us not be squeamish. The money that you'll be receiving from me won't come from greengrocers or cake shops. We both know there is always a component of human misery in a business like ours.'

'Please outline your proposal.' Igor sounded relaxed.

Erik shook his head and turned back to the cars. Sixteen, a blue car was inspected; fifteen, a green car. I reckoned he was less than a minute away from the van.

I would have to sacrifice myself to distract him from the cars. I had to draw his attention entirely onto me, and I could only hope that the consequences would not be too awful.

I took a deep breath, opened my mouth wide to shout his name . . . and then, from behind me, Helena's voice called instead.

Relief gushed through me. Helena was sacrificing herself! Erik spun round. I jammed myself harder against the tree, but then hesitated. Should I leap from amongst the branches to help Helena?

'The Bruins must go into exile,' Dad was saying.

'Exile?' Johann said. 'Hah! In exile they would have even more freedom to plot against the government.'

'Not if they came to me,' said Dad.

'To you?' Igor asked.

Erik left the cars and came to stand at the edge of the trees. He was no more than ten strides away.

'Send them to me,' Dad said. 'In exile they will go into hiding. The simple fact is that they will never come out of it.'

I wasn't breathing. I had my hand pressed over the walkie-talkie earpiece in case Erik could hear Dad's voice. Erik was in front of me. Helena was somewhere behind.

'You will kill them?' Johann's voice was hushed.

'I call it permanent exile.'

'I never thought. . . ' said Johann.

Erik was moving closer.

'It will ease the tensions at home,' Igor stated. 'If the Bruins remain in Domeria, they will be a permanent reminder. But if they disappear, it will be easy to make people believe that they are living a life of luxury somewhere remote and corrupt.'

Erik was four metres away and staring directly into my tree.

'Well, gentlemen, shall we say that our financial agreement begins the day that our problem is solved?' Dad asked.

'We will need to discuss this with our colleagues,' Johann said hurriedly.

'It must be finalised today,' Dad said.

'But . . .' said Johann.

'No discussion,' Igor cut him off. 'We have complete authority to act. You will have the Bruins within twenty-four hours.'

Erik was two metres from me. I had my hands pressed against the trunk ready to launch myself off and run. He moved, I readied myself, but he walked straight past. I turned to watch, preparing myself to leap to Helena's aid. I tensed to jump.

'Erik!' Helena hissed.

My heart seemed to stop beating as I heard her say in Domerian, '. . . videotaping Igor . . . Johann.'

I was dumbfounded. I had to be wrong. I could not
have heard Helena telling Erik we were videotaping
Igor and Johann.

Erik laughed. 'Videotaping?' he said.

'Isabella, . . . English . . .' Helena insisted. 'Video
camera, radio-mikes, walkie-talkies.' She thrust her
walkie-talkie at Erik.

I heard Dad's voice crackling from her walkie-
talkie and mine at the same time.

'We have a deal,' Dad was saying, 'Until
tomorrow then.'

Helena *had* said those words to Erik Booré.

Erik shrugged. 'Igor . . .' he said, and shook his
head. He didn't seem as upset as Helena. 'Amateurs!'
he laughed.

'. . . . . . video recording . . . Igor, Johann . . . Bruins.'

My legs were beginning to tremble from being
tensed in one position. I didn't dare shift my weight
for fear of discovery.

Erik laughed again. 'English amateurs!' he said.

I knew then that our videotape was in danger. I needed to tell Gary that Erik was coming for the tape. I was edging my finger towards the walkie-talkie button when Gary spoke.

'We've got it! We're done! Let's get out of here.'

The next moment I heard a squeal of tyres as the van swerved out of its parking place.

Helena cursed. I heard Erik punch some numbers and begin to talk on his mobile. I heard the words 'videotaping', 'blackmail' and 'amateurs' again.

'I will get the tapes,' Helena said in English. 'They don't suspect me. I can move freely among them.'

Erik finished his call. 'Make sure that they make no copies!' he said in English too.

I watched Helena walk away in the direction of General Wolfe. Erik disappeared amongst the trees. I heard the engine of the yellow car start up. Through gaps in the branches I watched Dad shake hands with Igor and Johann, climb into the car, and be driven away by Derek. No sooner was the yellow car gone than the black BMW car swooshed up beside Johann and Igor, and they sped away too.

I leaned back against the trunk and straightened my legs. Then, broken-hearted, I phoned Dad.

'Dad—'

'We did it, Isy!' he shouted. I could hear the sound of traffic around him.

'Dad, listen!'

'I was scared, Isy. So dangerous. But it worked!'

'Dad! Don't celebrate too soon!'

'You know, as we strolled out into the centre of that expanse of grass, an incredible calm——'

'Dad!' I hissed, trying to get his attention. 'Aunt Helena is a spy.'

'I beg your pardon!?'

'Aunt Helena. She was talking to Erik Booré. She's a spy for them. I think she's going to steal the videotape.'

'Not possible.'

'Totally possible. Totally true.'

There was silence as Dad absorbed the news.

'Oh my God, Isabella. I don't know . . . Look, Isy, I can't think at the moment, but don't tell anyone yet. We've got to think it through. Don't tell anyone . . . I mean, how come they didn't just cancel the meeting? This is too weird. Hang on——' I heard Derek's voice rumbling in the background. 'Isy, I've got to go. Helena! I can't believe it. I'll warn Gary. *Don't tell anyone else.*' The phone went dead.

I stayed under the tree for a while, watching and listening in case Erik, the agents or Helena were still around.

I couldn't believe it either! Her kidnapping must have been a fake. Her imprisonment in the black factory a fake too. Her escape from Mont Noir was a clever trick to fool us. And how many hundred lies had she told Leo while they were flying around the world and back?

I could see very little through the branches. I decided to phone Sam. Their walkie-talkie was probably still set on Channel Four.

'Have you seen Erik Booré?' I asked, as soon as she answered.

'He went out of the main gates five minutes ago with two men,' she said. 'Where are you?'

'Stuck under a tree near where the van was parked. Have you seen Helena?'

'Haven't seen her. Are you going to stay under your tree?'

'I'm coming out now,' I said.

'We'll wait for you at the park gates, then. And by the way, well done, Isy. Amazing.'

From beside the tree I made another inspection of the surrounding park. Time passed as two false alarms—Sunday strollers in dark hats and coats—sent me ducking back under the branches. I wondered where Otto and Helena were. Then, at last, I saw Helena down by General Wolfe, climbing into a black taxi. I rang Dad and told him Helena was on her way. When I hung up, my mobile rang almost straight away.

'It's me,' Leo said. 'Johann and Igor have just pulled up outside the airport. But I am phoning to ask, was it a success?'

'We've got a video of them making the deal.'

'Then they are going home to arrange my parents' release.'

'We'll know within twenty-four hours.'

'I have to go. They are entering the terminal. I'll phone again when they take off.' Leo was gone.

I had wanted so much to warn him about Helena. But Dad said not to. And how would Leo have reacted? He might have done something rash, like throw himself at Igor and Johann.

The field agents and Erik had left the park. Jane, Sam, and Alice were waiting for me at the gates. I had to assume that Dad, Derek, Patrice and Gary were back at the hotel. Helena would be at the hotel soon. Igor and Johann were about to take off for Domeria. Otto was the only one unaccounted for.

I phoned him.

'I'm on my way to London City Airport,' he said.

I told him that Igor and Johann had just arrived.

'My plane will wait until theirs has departed,' he explained. 'My pilot is on standby.'

'Good luck, Otto,' I said, the news of Helena hammering to get out of me. 'I hope to see you soon.'

I walked the long way round to get to Sam, Jane and Alice at the park gates. Then we split into pairs and went wandering to check if we were being followed, before walking back to the Clarence together.

We got back to the hotel without seeing either the field agents or Erik Booré. As we walked, we talked, and every time Helena's name was mentioned I had to battle the urge to tell them what I knew.

But the secret was still safe when Dad met us on the hotel steps. 'How you doing, guys?' he asked, cheerfully. 'Everyone's having lunch.'

'Helena too?' I asked, before I could stop myself. Dad flinched, but the others didn't seem to notice.

While I went up to wash my hands, Sam saved me the seat beside her, directly opposite Helena. I sat down, but couldn't bring myself to look across the table. I didn't know whether or not Helena was looking at me, but it felt as if the knowledge of her deceit was written all over my face. I couldn't trust my eyes not to give the game away.

A waiter placed a bowl of soup in front of me, and I kept my eyes fixed on it, listening to everyone chatting excitedly about the morning's events, and twitching every time the tape was mentioned.

I hadn't even touched my soup when the main courses arrived for everyone else. Dad had to open four bottles of wine that Nana had bought. I took a couple of sips of soup as desserts were served, but I had no appetite.

'I spoke to Otto at the airport,' I told them at one point, then clamped my mouth shut. It was a perfectly reasonable statement, but I suddenly wondered whether it might reveal important information to Helena.

'He's going home to look for Peter,' Patrice said. The sombre sound of his voice made me wonder whether he knew about Helena, too. But I could only guess.

'And where are Derek and Leo?' I asked Dad.

'Derek's taken the car back. He'll get his own car later. As for Leo . . . still at the airport, I suppose.'

'Hasn't he phoned?' I asked. 'He was going to phone me when . . .' I stopped again, wondering whether I was about to reveal something else. But Helena finished my sentence for me.

'Johann and Igor will have flown out by now,' she said. 'They'll be back in Domeria in a couple of hours.'

'He should have phoned, then,' I said. 'In fact, he should be here!' An image came into my head of Leo being surprised by the field agents at the terminal. Had Helena told Erik that Leo was at the airport?

Gary interrupted my thoughts. 'I'm off to set up the tape,' he said, pulling a videotape from inside his jacket. I glanced at the tape, then at him, then at Helena. Helena was staring at the tape. Had Dad forgotten to tell Gary?

'I'll be with you in a tick,' Dad said. 'When I've had a coffee.'

'And me,' Alice said.

'I want to look at my camera work,' said Patrice.

'I wasn't there at all,' said Nana, 'so I want a look.'

I wondered then if Dad had told them all.

When everyone had finished their meals, Helena and the others rose from the table. I stared at the tablecloth as they left the room. I still didn't trust my eyes.

Sam waited beside me.

'I'm going to phone Leo,' I said, pushing my soup aside and punching his number. 'He should have rung an hour ago.'

His phone was either switched off, or out of range. I hung up, not wanting to think how far out of range he might be. Drugged in a plane over France maybe?

I turned to Sam.

'Let's go and watch the video,' I said.

The curtains were closed, and everybody was crowded in a tight bunch around the TV when we entered Dad's room. Sam and I sat on the floor.

The screen brightened as the yellow car slid into view, and the tension in the room was high as we waited for Dad to utter his first words.

'*You Johann Feld?*' he asked.

Then the camera followed the three men as they strolled out into the centre of the open grass. Every word they spoke came through perfectly clear.

No-one made a sound as we watched the negotiations unfold.

'*I prefer to call it permanent exile*,' Dad was saying to the two men whose faces filled the screen.

'*We will need to discuss this with our colleagues*,' Johann said. I could see now how panicked he had been.

'*You will have the Bruins within twenty-four hours*.'

Igor had said the final words. Johann was shaking his head mutely as the camera tracked the three men back to Blackheath Avenue. Then the screen was filled with white lines.

There was a moment of silence. Then Dad laughed. We looked at him in surprise, and then we laughed too, except for Helena who was still staring at the screen.

'Well done, everybody,' Dad said. 'Thank God that's over. I think we can be proud of ourselves. Especially Isabella. But now that we've seen it, can everyone please head back down to the dining room again?'

Dad lead the way, followed by Jane, Sam, and Alice. Patrice gave his arm to Nana. Helena's gaze was still glued to the television screen, and mine was on the video-player in which our precious tape was still turning.

Gary grabbed his jacket from the back of a

chair. 'Come on Isy,' he said. 'Let's go and hear what else your dad's got to tell us.'

I scowled. Did he really want me to leave Helena alone with the tape?

'Let's go, Isy,' Gary said again.

'The tape is still in the video machine,' I mouthed.

He nodded, the tiniest dip of his head, then glared at me, grabbed me by the arm, and dragged me from the room.

'Helena's on their side,' I hissed, as soon as we were outside the door. I felt like shaking him.

'I know Isabella,' he grinned.

I was more befuddled than ever. Gary knew that Helena was a double agent, and Helena was now alone with the only recording of our work?

Gary stuck his head back into the room. 'Are you alright, Helena?'

'Yes . . . yes,' I heard her murmur. 'I am shocked.' Her words trailed away.

'I'll let you have a moment, then,' Gary said gently. 'Rewind the tape, and bring it down when you come.'

I managed to wait until Gary and I were halfway down the stairs.

'Please explain, Gary,' I said, 'before my brain explodes.'

'Technology, Isy,' he said. 'Satellite technology, transferring data digitally from a small grey van in

Greenwich Park to a friend's studio in Clapham. It's called back-up. Always back-up your data, Isy.'

Everyone was clustered at the back of the dining room except for Dad, who was standing at one of the windows, masked from outside by a floral curtain. He beckoned me over to stand behind him.

'Who knows about Helena?' I whispered.

'Only you, me and Gary,' he said. 'Watch!'

Dad pulled back the edge of the curtain so that I could see down into the carpark. We waited for several minutes, but nothing happened. Then suddenly, Helena was rushing down the front steps of the hotel clutching something to her breast. No sooner had she reached the edge of the road than a black BMW screeched to a halt, she climbed in, and with a squeal of tyres the car took off again. Erik Booré stared back at the hotel from the front passenger window as they drove away.

24

Sunday Afternoon

Our plans would have to change. Because Helena had betrayed our secrets and stolen the videotape, we knew that Johann and Igor weren't going to honour their side of the deal.

After we watched Helena leave, clutching what she thought was the only recording of the Greenwich Park negotiations, Dad told the others what I had discovered about her.

However, we still had something up our sleeve . . .

When the turmoil died down, Gary explained that we were in fact still in possession of the incriminating evidence. 'Come and have a gander at the final product,' he said.

Alice handed Gary a laptop computer, which he opened on a table. We gathered round while it booted up.

'Contained on this CD,' he said, 'is a copy of what we have just seen on the video upstairs, but with the face of one innocent person obscured.'

As he said this, a pixelated image of Dad's face

appeared on the screen between the sharp images of Johann and Igor.

'And as Isabella planned so brilliantly, we are going to send this little horror story,' he pointed to the computer screen, 'as an educational gift to the good people of Domeria.'

'I thought it would be a perfect way of telling them what their government is up to,' I explained.

'And when we're ready to distribute it,' Gary continued, as the Greenwich Park meeting played before our eyes yet again, 'I've organised a group of hackers here in London to feed these sounds and images onto as many Domerian sites that they can find. The hackers tell me that they have already identified seventy-eight Domerian government websites. Added to business and private websites, the number of places we can send the images to will run into thousands.'

'Why don't we send it now?' I asked.

Surely, the sooner we got the story out to the people of Domeria, the sooner the government would be toppled, and the sooner Leo's mum and dad would be released.

'We'll wait for Otto's word on that,' Gary answered. 'But within hours of me pressing the button, Domeria will be awash with the evidence of their finance minister and chief of security agreeing to do away with André and Theresa Bruin.'

'The people of Domeria will have to do the rest,' I said, crossing my fingers.

Dad's phone rang. He listened, then mouthed, 'Otto's just arrived at the Domerian border.'

All eyes turned to Dad.

'Kidnapped!' he suddenly cried. 'Oh *Leo*!'

Everyone groaned. Despite our very best efforts, it seemed Leo had managed to get himself abducted after all.

I went and stood beside Dad and tipped the phone away from his ear so that I could hear too.

'We haven't found Peter,' I heard Otto say. 'Saul is looking. And André and Theresa were just moved about an hour ago. I don't know where to. The rumour is the south. I suppose they're relocating them ready for transfer to England.'

I covered the mouthpiece of the phone and whispered, 'Doesn't Otto know about Helena?'

'I don't think so,' he whispered back.

'Should we tell him?'

Dad nodded, and said, 'Otto, I've got something to tell you . . . Helena is working with Erik Booré.'

'*What*!?'

'She was talking to him in the park,' Dad continued. 'Isabella heard it all.'

Then my phone rang. 'Isabella', a man's voice said. 'It is Peter. Let me talk to your father.'

'He's on the phone to Otto,' I said. 'Talk to me.'

'Tomorrow morning at seven. London City Airport. I have to go.'

'What?' I said, but he was gone.

Dad was saying, 'I didn't want to accept it either.'

'That was Peter,' I mouthed. 'And do we send the pictures yet?'

Dad relayed my question. 'Okay. We'll hear from you soon, then. Be safe.' He hung up.

'The news about Helena really upset his cool,' Dad said. 'And he doesn't want the pictures yet.'

'And Peter is out of prison,' I said. 'He wants us to meet him at London City Airport tomorrow morning. At seven.'

25

The Eleventh Day

Monday morning was bleak. I hoped the heavy rain, low clouds, and battering winds weren't going to upset plane arrivals.

It was five to seven, we'd parked Derek's car, and Gary, Alice, Dad and I were hurrying through the cold rain to the terminal. Around us, people in raincoats and umbrellas were doing the same. As we were about to step inside the front doors, a small man in a black trilby hat and a sodden raincoat barred our way.

In his dripping hand, written in black texta and protected by a film of plastic wrap, was a sign that read *MARTIN and ISABELLA*. We looked into his wet face. He looked back into ours. I didn't know what any of us was hoping to recognise, since I was sure we'd never met before.

He seemed to decide that we were the people he was looking for. He stuck his hand inside his coat and pulled out a small white envelope. Dad took the envelope, and the man walked quickly away and climbed into a grey car that immediately pulled out into the traffic.

We entered the terminal doors as Dad slit the envelope. Inside, was a slip of paper on which was printed the words '*WORLD NEWS*'.

'What!?' said Gary and Dad.

'Over there to the left,' I said, pointing to a newsagent shop with the words '*WORLD NEWS*' above it.

'Obviously we are to meet Peter in the newsagents,' said Alice, and hurried towards it.

We hung around for fifteen minutes, checking the headlines and the foreign news pages for any information on Domeria. There was nothing, and there was no sign of Peter either.

An announcement came over the terminal's loudspeakers.

'*Could passengers for Domeria, Isabella and Martin, please come to the airport information desk, situated on the left side of the terminal as you enter.*'

As soon as Dad showed his driver's licence to the woman at the information desk another envelope was handed over. Inside, the words on the slip of paper read '*MERIDIAN LINE*'.

'Meridian Line?' Dad asked the woman at the desk. 'Is that the nought degrees longitude line that runs through Greenwich Park?'

'Not Greenwich Park again!' I grumbled.

'It is also a restaurant on the first floor of this terminal,' she smiled.

'That's it, Dad! Come on!' I said, and rushed back to drag Alice and Gary from the newsagent.

The moment we stepped into the restaurant, my phone rang.

'I am sorry to lead you such a chase,' Peter said.

'Where are you?'

'In the terminal, like you. The various locations and the announcement were to ensure that you were not followed.'

'And why are we here?

'Wait a little longer and I will have the answer to that question, as well as a surprise for you.'

Horror, rather than surprise, was what I felt when, ten minutes later, I caught sight of Peter, Igor Mann and an unidentified man and woman heading towards the restaurant. I'd positioned myself near the entrance to catch the first glimpse of Peter, but I'd never dreamt that Igor Mann would be following him.

I sprinted to where Dad, Gary and Alice were sipping coffee at the back of the restaurant.

'Peter's here!' I hissed. 'And Igor Mann's following him!'

Alice's eyes grew wide as she looked over my shoulder. Then she, Dad and Gary rose slowly to their feet. I turned to see Peter and Igor enter the restaurant.

'The big man's Peter,' I whispered.

But Peter didn't have his hands in the air as I'd expected, given that Igor Mann was behind him. Could Peter have changed sides again?

A man who I thought I recognised from a picture in the Domerian newspaper was with them. He was tall, with a lean face and longish grey hair, which was pushed back from his forehead. Beside him was a tall slim woman, about mum's age, with her black hair pulled into a neat French roll.

I tried to run through the possibilities: Igor Mann hadn't been alerted to our trick by Erik or Helena, and was keeping to the plan for the disposal of Leo's parents. Or perhaps the man and woman were *pretending* to be Leo's parents, and Igor had brought them along to make us think that the plan was still going ahead? But why, if Igor knew of our trick, had he even pretended to bring Igor's parents?

But maybe if Helena and Erik and Igor didn't know that *we* knew that *they* knew that the plan was a trick. After all, we'd apparently trusted Helena enough to give her the opportunity to steal the video. Was Igor still in pursuit of our organisation?

But why was Peter so relaxed? He had originally been my enemy, then he'd become my ally. Had he become an enemy again?

Then Peter gave a friendly wave. Dad gulped,

indicated that we should stay where we were, and began walking towards the four of them. Gary and Alice stayed put, but I tagged along.

'Martin,' Igor said.

Dad replied in his gang-leader's voice. 'The Bruins?' he asked.

Dad was probably doing the exact same wondering that I was.

'Let me make some introductions,' Igor said to Dad, and proceeded to introduce us to Peter and the Bruins—if that's who they really were.

I caught Peter's eye and nodded. Dad didn't know what to do.

'We have a great deal to be grateful to you for,' said the man who probably wasn't André.

'How can we ever thank you?' the woman added. 'You and your family have helped us so much.'

'And Helena too, unhappily,' said the man.

Dad blinked. Like me, he was probably trying to work out what was meant by 'Helena too, unhappily'. If these people really were André and Theresa, then the fact that Helena was a double agent would probably have been kept from them. If they *weren't* really André and Theresa, then they wouldn't have revealed that they knew that Helena was on the government's side.

I couldn't work it out. I don't think Dad could either. He studied the floor, looked at Peter, looked at Igor, and looked back to where Alice and Gary were standing.

Igor smiled. 'Let me put you out of your misery, Martin,' he said.

Dad eyed Igor warily.

'Helena was not the only double agent involved in this conspiracy,' Igor explained. 'You know about Peter's role, of course, but I too have been working for the opposite side.'

I gasped.

Dad looked doubtful. His brain must have been going a million to the dozen. 'But why was Helena kidnapped, then?' he asked.

'I told Erik Booré to do it,' Igor answered. 'I pretended that I needed to debrief Helena face to face.'

Dad was still doubtful. 'But why are André and Theresa here if Helena revealed our Greenwich Park plot to Erik Booré?' he said. 'Why did the government release them, if the incriminating videotape is now in the government's hands?' His gangster act had completely disappeared.

'Helena phoned me and told me it was a trick, but I kept that information to myself. But when Erik told Johann, and Johann told his fellow ministers, they panicked. So when I suggested that André and Theresa be moved to somewhere much more remote and secure they agreed at once. I omitted to tell them that the new place of detention was a private airstrip in the south of Domeria.'

Dad glanced at the man and woman. 'Somewhere remote maybe, but why are they here in England?'

'For their own safety, Martin. The politics of Domeria are in turmoil. Friends and foes can be indistinguishable.'

'We will enjoy a couple of days being at a safe distance from the politics of Domeria,' the man said.

Like me, Dad was wavering. The Bruins were nodding.

'We were also most anxious,' the woman continued, 'to meet the two people who have risked their lives for us and, more importantly, the nation of Domeria.'

'Please,' André said quietly, 'let me assure you that the people who stand before you are André and Theresa Bruin, the parents of Leo. I look forward to the day very soon when Leo will also be free to thank you.'

'So where is Leo?' I asked.

'We think we know where he is. We think he is safe, but . . .' the woman smiled bleakly.

'It is time to send the information, then,' said Igor. 'It is time to flood the computer screens of Domeria. As for you, Isabella,' he smiled, 'I have Security Service employment papers for you to sign any time you like.'

26

More Holidays

That afternoon Nana insisted that she return home to her flat in Blackheath, and that Dad and I accompany her. Sam, Jane, Gary and Alice decided it was time to start their real lives again.

On Tuesday, Nana, Dad and I went to see a lot of famous people made of wax at Madame Tussauds. Then we were spun around on a giant Ferris wheel called the London Eye; followed by a gaze through the railings of Buckingham Palace. That night there was a party with Nana's side of the family.

On Wednesday we visited the National Gallery and the British Museum. And that night, everyone from Dad's father's side of the family came over.

We bought three London papers every day, and watched the news every evening. But there was no news about Domeria.

On Thursday we walked to the Maritime Museum in Greenwich Park. I didn't know what to feel, walking through that park again. A memory of fear, and a sense of satisfaction, perhaps. I did know that our minds were never far from Domeria.

Someone phoned to tell us that André and Theresa had flown to Belleau. Close enough to Domeria for when they were needed, but far enough away to preserve their safety. We were still waiting for news of Leo.

It was Friday, and I was in my pyjamas, enjoying a leisurely breakfast, when Dad burst in through the front door.

'Look at this!' he shouted, his eyes gleaming as he held up an inside page of a newspaper. **'DOMERIANS MARCH FOR DEMOCRACY'** was printed across the top.

'Read it,' Dad said, thrusting it at me.

It talked about a march—a mass movement, the journalist called it—sweeping down Highway One to the capital. But most importantly, it said that André Bruin was in the lead.

It also gave a detailed account of the history and politics of Domeria, and a vivid description of the people who swarmed to the foot of Mont Bruin to join the march and talked about a sophisticated Internet Campaign flooding the computer screens of Domeria.

'Sophisticated Internet Campaign, eh?' Dad said, patting me on the arm. I patted him back on the head.

Later that day we cruised up the River Thames,

me with the newspaper report folded neatly inside my jacket. Nana pointed out Tower Bridge, with its roadway that lifted up to let ships through, and its five-pointed towers on each end. We visited the Tower of London on the bank of the river, where traitors were once imprisoned and tortured and had their heads chopped off. I thought of a certain woman in Domeria. We were on our way home when Dad saw the headline at Charing Cross Station:

'ARMY TANKS MASS AGAINST MARCHERS'.

It was splayed right across page one of the *Evening Standard*. My heart sank to my knees, then sank to my ankles when Dad read from the report.

'"In a dangerous turn of events for the Domerian Democratic Party",' Dad read, '"the eleven tanks of the Armoured Division of the Domerian Army have halted the march that seemed set to carry André Bruin into Domeria City and into power."'

'One tank would be enough,' said Nana grimly.

'Listen to this,' Dad said, scanning down the page. '"The Domerian government is now arguing that the widespread Internet campaign is a conspiracy created by the DDP and its foreign allies."'

'Blaming our organisation again!' I said.

'". . . and that they will do whatever is necessary to halt the illegal protests and restore order."' Dad slapped the newspaper with the back of his hand.

The train journey back to Nana's was silent and bleak. Dad kept reading and re-reading the article to himself. Maybe he was hoping that it would change magically into good news.

The evening at Nana's was bleak too. Dad listened to the radio in the kitchen while he ate, while Nana and I sat in the dining room. Then we surfed for hours through the television channels, looking for breaking news.

Television Channel Four had the story, but they only showed pictures of the snow-capped Lodo Mountains with the words 'file footage', underneath.

At two o'clock, after watching the fourteenth repeat of the story, we gave up and went to bed.

I was woken two hours later by Dad shouting from the lounge room. 'Isy! Mum! Come and look! Quick! Come and look, now!' I stumbled out of bed to see what was wrong. Nana was already transfixed by the television. On the screen, the file footage of the Lodo Mountains was being transmitted once again, but this time with a crackling voiceover.

'In an extraordinary reversal of political fortune, Helena Benz, a close friend and political ally of André Bruin, has earned herself a place in Domerian history,' the voiceover said.

'As their most terrible traitor,' Nana murmured.

'As the standoff continued between the tanks and the unarmed supporters of André Bruin, and a bloody confrontation seemed inevitable, Helena Benz appeared out of the crowd and climbed onto the turret of the leading tank.'

'She was going to help them shoot at the marchers,' I said.

'Ssh!' Dad said angrily.

'Addressing those closest to the tanks, she spoke about her recent presence in England at secret negotiations for the murder of André and Theresa Bruin. Despite the vast crowd, Ms Benz's words were passed person to person along the mile-long line of seated marchers. As her words reached each of them, the marchers rose to their feet.'

'A mile-long line of marchers,' I repeated, imagining the great stream of people.

'She said that the Domerian Government she had once served . . .'

'Once served?' Nana asked. 'I'll believe that when—'

'. . . and had given orders to halt this democratic march, was also arranging to sell the lives of the Bruins, as well as the future of the Domerian people, to a gang of London criminals.'

'The Greenwich Gang,' Dad mumbled.

'This correspondent then watched with dread as the Commander of the Tank Division spoke into his microphone. Then the day was shattered by the sound of a tank engine starting, then another, then a third, fourth and fifth, until all eleven tanks were roaring and belching diesel smoke into the sky.'

'Oh my God!' I said.

'Then the tanks began to move. The marchers watched in stunned silence as the tanks turned away from the protesters and began to roll down the mountain pass to lead the marchers to the capital.'

We cried.

I was still awake when my phone rang at six.

A shout came down the phone. 'Isabella!'

'Leo!' I shouted back.

'We are in Domeria City! The government has run away!'

'Y-e-e-e-sss!' I shouted, punching the air. Dad and Nana stumbled in.

'But Helena?' I asked.

'She saved our lives. Because of Helena, we are here in the city, Isabella. I am sitting on the gun turret of a tank, and the square and all the streets are filled with people celebrating . . . I wish you were here. This is because of you.' There was a roar as a tank started its engine. 'I have to go,' Leo shouted over the roar. 'I will phone again tomorrow.'

That night the television news showed

thousands of people pouring into Domeria City Square. Above them, high on the balcony of a grand building, were André, Theresa and Leo Bruin.

* * *

We had planned a three week holiday in England. But almost before the holiday began, the first eleven days of it were stolen away.

Eleven days.

I suppose it was my fault they were stolen. Maybe I should learn not to talk to strangers quite so much. Maybe Dad and I shouldn't have minded what was happening to Leo and Helena.

But then I am reminded of what Leo said to me on the plane over Afghanistan.

'You are not allowed *not* to care, Isabella.'

And I have to say I agree with him. Absolutely.